AGAINST OWL ODDS

OWL STAR WITCH MYSTERIES BOOK 8

LEANNE LEEDS

Against Owl Odds
ISBN: 978-1-950505-69-2
Published by Badchen Publishing
14125 W State Highway 29
Suite B-203 119
Liberty Hill, TX 78642 USA

CONTENTS

AGAINST OWL ODDS

CHAPTER ONE

"You can't bring that owl in here," the Gothic-themed blond at the door snapped at me. She scowled and brandished her pink sparkle fingernails in my face in full drama queen mode. "There are no pets allowed in *Sanguine*. None." The loud music thumped behind her in a soundtrack of techno beat and bass. "You need to bring that thing somewhere else. This isn't a Harry Potter cosplay party, you know."

"Can I bite her face off?" Archie asked, insulted. He harrumphed indignantly and squeezed my shoulder with his talons, and leaned down until he almost touched me with his beak. "She knows that a vampire owns this place, right?

I mean, he's half a pet, right?" The owl waited for me to respond, but I just raised an eyebrow. "The bat thing? Bats can be pets, right?"

"Ma'am, why are you not leaving?" the goth girl asked, her attitude growing even more snotty. "This is a private fundraiser, and I'm sure we don't have any owls on the list."

I ignored her question and responded with one of my own. "Is Rex around?" I asked as she tapped her foot in the impossibly high-heeled shoes she wore. (Or, I guess you could call them boots since they were up to her knees and laced up the front.)

"Show her your teeth, Morticia!" one of the other women called from behind the door podium. "She's totally hot for you. Just give her some fang; she'll be yours."

"Shut up, Twinkle! You think you're so slick!" Morticia snarled over her shoulder. She swung back around to glare at me. "I'm serious, dude. We have no pets allowed. I will have the bouncer forcibly remove you and then call the police. You need to leave."

"If you even try to—"

"Astra!" Rex's voice cut across the front entrance like a whip. "It's about time you got here!" Rex appeared at the door with a big smile, his arms outstretched. I stepped over the threshold and into a cold hug from Emma's vampire brother. "Your sister's already in the back doing readings for the attendees. But, you know, if you charge a few bucks to hold Archie, we might raise even more money."

"My apologies, but my schedule is packed with better things," Archie told him with a shrug of his wings and a roll of his eyes.

Morticia's face contorted in a grimace as we spoke, and her ordinarily pristine pale white skin mottled into a snapshot of rage. She spat out a string of vile curses under her breath, but Rex waved away her tirade with a bored look.

Morticia's face flushed a deeper red as she whirled to stomp away.

"She doesn't like to be wrong. Do you, Tish?" Twinkle called after her, laughing. "That girl is more slippery than a pocket full of pudding."

"Do you make sure they have the right screw-you attitude before coming to work here, or is it something you teach them?" I asked Rex as he took me into his big club beside the motorway. With each step toward the back of the building, the volume intensified, and I had to yell to be heard.

"I only hire the best, Astra," Rex said with a

grin. He slipped his arm around my shoulders. "Born with it, or taught it. Are you sure you don't want to hire on? I can make you a partner. How awesome would that be? A vampire and a witch own a disco club. There's a story there, I'm sure of it."

I followed Rex through the chamber until I came to a courtyard with marble tiled pillars, benches, and a low fountain in the patio center. Ami was in the corner, counseling one of the countless inebriated and rowdy fundraiser guests who, no doubt, would not remember a word of her advice the following day.

"I'm pleased we're no longer at odds, Rex, but I doubt you and I as business partners would be a smart idea in any capacity," I replied as the vampire brought me a blue and white frozen drink with a yellow umbrella in it. "Besides, I enjoy my job at the police department, and your sister is available during the day. So there's that."

He laughed and nodded.

We were leaning against a massive, round marble bar built from the exterior wall. It was mirrored, with a bartender dressed in black leather pants, boots, and a silver bow tie. I doubted anyone else noticed he was a vampire with a black beard and long hair pulled back in a ponytail. Still, I saw the pointy fangs he did a fantastic job concealing.

"So, what's the fundraiser for again?"

Rex smiled. "The Forkbridge Blood Bank."

I nearly choked on my pretty blue tropical drink.

* * *

"THANK YOU, thank you, thank you for coming!"

A woman I faintly remembered as some sort of society maven interrupted the Duran Duran cover band in the middle of their set and took the microphone. "As an FBB supporter, you already know our community's challenges each day, ensuring patients at local hospitals have the blood and platelet transfusions they need to live."

The audience applauded—rather inappropriately, I may add. Patients who do not have blood are not something anyone should cheer for. But they were inebriated, and their eighties fueled exhilaration got the best of them.

"Hey," my middle school teacher boyfriend, Jason, said in my ear as he slid next to me. "I apologize for being late; the meeting at the school ran over." He kissed me on the cheek and scratched Archie's head in greeting. "I hope I did not miss anything."

"Only if you like Duran Duran," I said, nodding toward the twenty-somethings dressed like they had some firsthand knowledge of the eighties.

Which they didn't.

"Along with the increase in patients in need of blood and platelet transfusions, our hospital and healthcare system has been victimized repeatedly by whole blood donation theft," the woman reminded the crowd. They let out a loud *oooh* in response. "This year, FBB is fundraising with the help of Sanguine—and our valued supporter Rex Sullivan—to add the critical equipment and services necessary to meet the growing need for blood and platelet transfusions in our community. In addition to that—with your generous donations—we'll be able to upgrade our security system and bring an end to the thefts plaguing our organization!"

"Yeah, not likely," a man whispered under his breath as he passed by the bar.

"Thank you very much for attending, and please, give generously! Now, I return the stage to Notorena!" The woman gestured toward the paunchy Simon LeBon-esque lead singer.

"Notorena?" I asked out loud.

"It's a combination of *Notorious* and *Arena*. Two Duran Duran albums."

I stared at Jason. "You didn't even google that."

"I did not."

"To Sanguine and to the FBB!" Notorena called out before they began to play *Girls on Film*. Strobe lights flashed.

"To Sanguine and the FBB!" everyone repeated, lifting their drinks in response.

I turned back to Jason, who had taken a seat next to me at the bar, and asked, "So, does this count as a date if you're late? I want to make sure this counts as a date. Emma's counting how many we've had. In fact, she and I kind of have a bet going."

"A bet?"

I nodded, sipping my melted blue...thing. "She thinks we don't go out enough to have a healthy relationship. She says we can't get our average up to once a month if you consider our track record —and discount all of the crazy Cocoa Beach mermaid murder thing. I think she's wrong."

"Huh. I feel a little insulted. I think we have a perfectly healthy relationship," Jason said as he leaned away from a staggering man waving a fistful of dollar bills at the bow-tied bartender.

"We see each other every morning for our run, and we get together in the evening when we can. At least once a week. Maybe not formal dates, but, I mean, we do." He winced and frowned as the staggering man elbowed him sharply in the ribs. "Though I might call this evening more of an obligation than a date."

"Buddy, you want to be careful who you slam into?" I snapped across the bar, glaring at the man. His watery, unfocused eyes scanned around wildly and finally found me. "You just elbowed my boyfriend in the ribs. Watch it, will you?"

The guy snorted. "He doesn't seem to care, lady. Stay in your backyard. Besides, I didn't bump into anyone. You imagine things." His head swiveled back toward the bartender.

I stiffened, ready for a confrontation.

"Astra, just let it go," Jason told me, his tone gentle and his eyes apologetic. "I know that you're not used to people that don't need to be rescued, but I'm fine. I don't need to be rescued."

"Just because it's a club doesn't mean people shouldn't—

"Astra, I'm fine."

I glared at the drunk guy again and gave him a mental kick.

He jumped as if the bar had shocked him and

immediately turned to face me. "You got a problem, lady?" he demanded, his voice rising.

"Friend, it's a fundraiser, and you're a little drunk." Jason stood up and stepped in front of me. "How about everybody just calm down?"

"She started it!"

I lifted my eyebrow and stared him down. The drunk guy was young and had a buzz cut and a crooked nose. He looked like he'd been in a fight before, so maybe he had fighting experience. I glanced down and thought I saw a knife outline at his waist.

Eh, didn't matter.

I could take him.

I stood up.

"You know he felt that, right, Astra?" Archie asked me. "Jason's not hurt, and that guy is so sloshed he's probably not even following what you're saying."

"Felt what?" I asked Archie without taking my eyes from the man.

Archie glowered. "Don't mentally zap people."

Oh.

Oops.

On instinct, I willed the confrontational sot to weave his way to the furthest chair away from us.

Sure enough, he did just that without another word to either Jason or me.

"Better," Archie mumbled.

"So," Jason said, sliding back next to me at the bar, "about this bet?"

"It's stupid. Emma's just being stupid. And nosy."

He frowned. "How did this whole thing come up, anyway?"

"She thinks it's more than just not dating like normal people. She's convinced we're avoiding the sparkle elephant in the room."

He laughed—but stopped when he caught the serious expression on my face. " I don't understand. What elephant?"

"Our relationship." I cleared my throat and leaned forward. "You know." His expression said he clearly did not. I sighed. "That you're a human and I'm a witch, and generally, those types of relationships don't work out all that well." I looked up at him. "Oh, come on, Jason. Have you not noticed that I live in a house full of women?"

"I have."

"Four sisters and none of us ever talk about our fathers? Grandfathers?"

"I have noticed that, too," Jason admitted. "I

figured if you wanted to discuss it with me, you'd bring it up when you were ready."

The band finished their song, and the crowd clapped.

Jason took my hand and squeezed it tight. "Astra, whatever we have to work through, whatever we have to discuss, whatever we need to deal with, I have the utmost confidence that we can work through anything. That we can talk about anything. I'm not worried." He half-smiled. "I grew up in Cassandra. I may have wanted a normal life once—but I certainly realized that was always unlikely for me."

"If you say so." I shrugged, unable to shake my misgivings.

Notorena started up again with a romantic rendition of *Save a Prayer*. Jason pulled me toward the dance floor and into his arms.

"Now it's a date," he whispered in my ear as we swayed among the drunk patrons holding cell phone flashlights up like we were attending a Duran Duran concert in Orlando. "Emma can stuff it."

* * *

"OKAY, sis, go for it. Tell me about it," I said, resting my chin on my hand.

Ami shuffled her cards, her poker face ruined by her scowl. "You're concerned about your relationship," Ami murmured. She picked through her tarot deck on the small table, candlelight shimmering between us.

"I'm worried about our relationship a bit, but not how your judgmental scowl indicates you think I am," I admitted. "It's more about our longevity than anything else."

"Because he's human?" she asked. Then, trying to hide the smirk tugging at her mouth, she added, "Or because he's awesomely hot and you don't make much time for him, and you're worried he's going to find some perky human girl that will."

"Ha. Ha."

"Sorry, I had to." The smile faded. "Okay, seriously."

I shook my head, looking back down at the cards. "Honestly, I don't know that I love him," I admitted. "And if I don't, is it fair to make him work on this at the level he'll probably need to? Start dealing with all that stuff? I mean…I don't know."

"Don't know what?"

I paused. "If I love him."

"You said that twice."

"I did."

"And I hear you."

"I'm surprised you can hear anything in this damn place," Archie grumbled, shifting his weight to one foot and rustling his feathers. "Why do they have the music turned up so high? The Hiereiai weren't this loud, and they were trying to make sure their chanting was heard on Olympus."

Hiereiai was the title of the female priesthood or priestesses in ancient Greek religion (being the equivalent of the male title Hierei.) Archie, the divine owl, liked to drop these little nuggets on us to remind us he was ancient and could name drop Greek gods going way back.

"It's a human thing," Ami told him distractedly, her eyes still on mine. "No one says you have to fall in love with Jason right now, Astra. There's no set rule for when that happens or how fast it has to happen. And isn't it up to him if he wants to be married to a witch? It's not your decision. It's his. Talk about what you want to talk about. Ask what you want to ask."

"Sometimes, it doesn't even feel like it's fair to ask." I bit my lip. "I know that I'm becoming a more…relaxed person when I'm around him, but I'm afraid that the opposite is true for him. I'm afraid that I'm becoming…I don't know—"

"Are you done?"

When I looked up, a vampire was staring at me, the candlelight flickering in his eyes, making them appear angry red. With a black-gloved hand on his hip, he scowled down at me. "Excuse me?"

"There's a line of people waiting for tarot card readings. But, unfortunately, you've decided your piddling five-dollar donation allows you to monopolize the reader's entire evening." He raised a finger to point at me. "I'm next, and you're taking entirely too long."

Archie drew himself up to his full height and ruffled his wings.

The vampire turned to glare at him. "What?"

"You are aware that a certain amount of charity goes along with the privilege of participating, correct? Or did you just show up here to find your next victim?"

"I'm incredibly aware," he said, his voice tight and nostrils flaring.

I blinked, shocked the vampire could hear Archie talk. "Can everybody hear you now?" I whispered, raising an eyebrow.

Archie shrugged.

Turning back to Ami, I leaned forward. "We can continue this when I see you at home," I told her. "I wouldn't want to ruin Fangs McMeany's evening."

"And who might you be to call me names?" The vampire glared at me. "Considering your brazen and impertinent rudeness, I would hope you are someone of consequence." A tiny hiss escaped his blood red lips. "It's a shame to watch people fall after reaching above their station."

"My sister," Ami said, standing up beside me. "And unless you want me to have you thrown out—"

"Not possible, and if she is your sister, you can see her some other time." The vampire threw twenty dollars down on the table with a huff. "Her and her feathered, birdbrained friend here." The vampire turned back to glare at me, his eyes glittering with irritation. "Both of you will step aside and let me have my turn."

I stood up, my own anger getting the better of me. "I don't know who you think you are, but—"

"I am Damien Elkhart, an old one and part-owner of this establishment, and with that"—he pointed to the money—"I have contributed enough to your charity for the evening," the vampire said, rolling his eyes. "If you would like to be so kind as to vacate that seat so I can get what I paid for, perhaps I will not see fit to throw *you* out of this place on your quite ample keister."

"I'm not going anywhere." I crossed my arms, my stomach turning with anger. "And Rex Sullivan owns Sanguine. Not you."

I could see the vampire's eyes flash in the candlelight, his face going even more pale than normal. "I don't appreciate your tone, witch."

"I don't appreciate yours."

The vampire stared at me for a moment, his face contorting with anger. "I've half a mind to—"

"Astra, let me just do his reading, and then he can go." Ami touched my arm. "Okay?"

I took a deep breath and looked away from the vampire. "Okay."

"Thank you," Ami told Damien as she sat down by the table again. "And, for the record, you're insulting."

"Did your cards tell you that? Don't think I'm unaware of who you are," the vampire growled, his voice dropping to a menacing whisper. "You will give me my reading, and then I will find some human who can entertain me."

"Okay, let's get this over with," she muttered, shuffling the cards in her hands.

"What are you doing?" The vampire slammed

his hand on the table, his face turning dark red. "You're shuffling incorrectly."

Ami glanced up at him, her eyes becoming hard and cold. "I'm sorry?"

"What's wrong with you? You're shuffling the cards wrong."

"You think you know better than I do?" Ami asked, her brows furrowing and her voice turning low.

"It was just an observation."

Ami brought the deck down onto the table, flicked her wrist, and cut the deck. The cards sprayed across the table, and she grabbed them with her right hand, flipped a few over, and spread the rest out in front of her with her left. It was a good mix: aces and a few court cards, but I could see that my sister somehow knew they were not what she was looking for yet. Her fingers ran over the card, her face showing confusion.

I glanced at the vampire and saw he was sitting stock still, watching Ami with curiosity and irritation. "I just need to know if the woman I love will finally come to her senses and realize that she and I are meant to be together." He narrowed his eyes. "This isn't rocket science."

"If she's decided you're not for her, I'd say she

already came to her senses," Archie muttered from my shoulder.

"I see a woman in the cards, but she's not in love with you," Ami said, her voice trance-like, as if she were looking at something far away. "Your love isn't returned. At least not by her." She jerked her head back. "There are three people here. Two men and one woman—you're the man. She's the woman." My sister looked up at Damien. "Is she with someone else? Someone you both know?"

"Yes," Damien said, his voice softer now, his anger fading. "Yes, she is."

"Are you in love with the man or the woman?"

"The woman, you idiot," he snapped, his arrogant attitude boiling over once more. "But that selfish jerk is ruining everything. And it should be me, not him."

Boy, this guy is a real prize, I thought.

Ami's eyelids flickered, and she appeared to be on the edge of collapsing. She took a deep breath and clutched the table's edge for support. "You will have to decide whether you're willing to let her go," she said, her voice still sounding distant. "If you love her, you'll have to let her go. Or something terrible could happen."

"That's easy for you to say." He pointed his

finger at Ami. "She is mine. We belong together. You don't know anything."

"Let me pull one more card. Maybe it'll be clearer. Maybe this will clear things up," Ami said, a note of uncertainty creeping into her voice as she shuffled. Then, holding the deck out to him, he pulled a card and held it out to her.

She flipped the card over.

"Oh, no," Ami gasped.

"Uh oh," Archie muttered. The glow from Athena's star card bathed our faces in a gentle, divine light. "This could be tricky." The bird cocked his head. "Isn't he technically already dead?"

"You must be kidding me," I said to Ami. "Is this a joke?"

She shook her head no, her eyes glued to the glowing card.

The goddess Athena decided *this* schmuck needed saving?

Ami looked up at the vampire and then back down at the card, but she didn't say anything to Damien at all. Instead, she stared at it for a few seconds, like she was waiting for it to change, and then finally looked up at me. "I'm so sorry."

"That's it?" Damien asked, misunderstanding Ami's apology. Standing up, fury blooming on his face, he added, "That's the best you can do? You're a sham. You can't even give me a decent reading. I've heard better from children than from you."

Ami got up from the table, shoved the star card into my hand, and walked away from the table, leaving Damien and me alone.

"I didn't dismiss you, young lady! I'm not done complaining! What happened?" he asked me, his anger shifting to confusion. "What's wrong with her?"

Seriously?

I looked down at the card, the star's multicolored rays pointing out in all directions. "Let's sit down. I'll be happy to explain it to you."

CHAPTER TWO

*D*amien Elkhart was a handsome vampire—which was pretty standard for vampires, actually. Something about the human-to-bloodsucker transformation worked better than a Queer Eye makeover, changing even the nerdiest, overweight human into a lanky, toned vampire with a patrician, noble-birthed air about them.

He smelled like blood and attraction, a heady combination of sweat and rain and human musk, a powerful and dark scent that was almost a tangible force against the senses. Elkhart's voice had the same coolness as his skin, low and deep and a little too smooth—but strong. Damien barely had to raise his voice to be heard over *Ordinary World*.

Unfortunately, it was a voice used to issuing commands and having them obeyed (or flinging insults and having people cower.) Nevertheless, the vampire's expression told me that was precisely what he expected from me.

Fat chance.

Despite my clearly explaining what the star card meant, how it signified his life was in danger, and how our chance meeting with the glowing card meant the goddess Athena wanted him to continue living, he seemed unconcerned.

"Do you have any questions?" I asked.

Damien's gaze darted around the room, surveying the humans as if he were searching for a dog toy at a pet store, lingering on those with abundant blessings in the chest area.

"Damien?"

"Yes, yes, I heard you. Your goddess doesn't necessarily want me to survive," Damien said distractedly, turning back to face me. "Gods are capricious things. Maybe she's got a vengeful bone to pick with whoever wants to kill me, and she just wants to make you jump through hoops to find them." Damien's eyes turned an icy shade of blue, and he lifted a hand toward me. "Perhaps she's just using me. I sense she's already had a good run at using you."

I frowned. "I'm not here to defend what's happening or explain it beyond what I've told you. You'll note that I am not the goddess."

He snorted with laughter. "Clearly."

"I am the avatar of the goddess—which means I'm the mouthpiece, not the brain," I told him through clenched teeth. "I can't say why she wants you to survive, but that card means she does." He looked away again. "Though considering how sadistic and self-centered you come off, I have no idea why she would come to that conclusion."

The insult made him whip back around and turn even colder, the anger inside him building, his black eyes darkening. I didn't need a digital readout to know that his blood pressure was rising as his heart rate increased.

"I don't need your help or your protection, woman. You," he said, emphasizing the word, "are the last person on this earth I'd ever let protect me."

"The last person? The *very* last person? Well, golly, mister vampire, sir, that just breaks my heart," I told him snidely. Archie made a hissing sound and clutched my shoulder tighter, his dislike for Damien palpable. "So, I have to ask. Is it because I'm a woman or a witch?"

Damien's lips thinned into a hard, mocking line. "It's because I don't need any help, you insolent lapdog. I'm a killer. I'm an apex predator. I follow no one. Witch, woman, priestess, whatever. I don't need anyone's help. I certainly don't need yours."

Archie clicked his beak as he perched on my shoulder as if even more annoyed by the vampire's words. The bird had been silent—words-wise, anyway—since Damien and I started our exchange, and the owl was doing exactly zip to help me.

I leaned forward and put a hand on the table, fixing him with a hard stare, letting him see the same sort of antipathy and purpose *I* was feeling. "Look, you overbearing tick—the goddess wants you to survive this, whatever it is. I'm here to make sure you do. That means we will work together on that. Just that."

"Are you deaf? I don't need your help," Damien said, his voice quiet but full of venom. He clenched his fists under the table, the tendons in his neck tightening. "I don't need anyone's help."

I sat back and held up my hands. "Then you're

going to die," I said flatly. I stood up and headed for the bar, leaving the vampire in his seat.

I wouldn't continue arguing with him; it chafed against my professional sensibilities. The only power I had over him was the divine mandate. So I would not argue with him or force him to cooperate with me. I was well past the point of threatening him or pleading with him. I didn't think either would change his mind.

So, I'd work around him. I'd done it before.

Since we were at a gathering with a plethora of vampires, I may as well gather intel.

* * *

I TOOK a seat at the bar and signaled the bartender. Chesty McBowtie came over and gave me a casual smile, his fangs glinting in the flashing lights. "What can I get you, Ms. Arden? Another Frostbite?"

"No, thanks," I replied, my hands gripping the stool. I forced a smile. "Do you know Damien Elkhart?"

"Damien Elkhart?" He frowned and looked around the room, scanning to see if anyone was close enough to overhear. (Which was ironic— vampires had incredible hearing. Every vamp in the place knew every word Damien and I said to each other. Including this bartender.) "He spends a lot of time here," he said cautiously.

"Do you think he could be in trouble?" I asked, keeping my tone light.

The bartender leaned forward and rested his arms on the bar, fixing me with a stern look. "Our kind tends to get a little concerned when people start asking questions," he said. "Especially about other vampires. There's a lot of...politics and such that go into being a vampire. You worked in Imperatorial City. You know."

"Gotcha," I said. "Just a friendly inquiry." I shrugged nonchalantly. "I'm interested in why he's here. He seems a little... well, out of place. That's it. I'm not asking you to break your blood oath or anything. I'm trying to do my job."

"Why do you want to know about Damien?" Rex asked, appearing out of nowhere. "Why don't you help those folks down at the end of the bar, Jake." Rex's suggestion to the bare-chested Jake was not a suggestion.

The bartender cleared his throat, moved down the bar, and fawned over a couple of women who looked like they were there to be fawned over.

I looked at Rex but didn't answer. He looked like he had something on his mind.

Rex glanced around the room. "Look, Astra, I don't mean to be rude," he said, leaning forward so that only I could hear him. "But this bar is neutral ground. So that means if anyone here thinks you're a threat to anyone in the room—and Damien is someone who would be particularly sensitive to that—you'll cause me a lot of problems and possibly wind up followed home by a bunch of vampires."

"They'd get a bit more than they bargained for," I told him arrogantly. "You know what just happened—I know all of you heard the conversation. And you, Rex? Your sister has to have told you enough about the star card that you know I'm no threat to Damien. Maybe they don't, but you do."

In the Venn diagram of vampire and witch worlds, while they were both in the same general paranormal world area, our societies had little overlap. Vampires had hierarchies and protocols, a whole Alice-in-Wonderland absurdity of complicated laws that bound them—much of which they didn't inform the rest of us about. A good portion of which they didn't bother to follow.

Witches, in general, didn't give an owl pellet about what happened to or in the vampire world —well, unless it affected the human world. Or the witch world. Or the paranormal world.

On those occasions, we had a tendency to meddle.

Conversely, I doubted the vampires knew much about my Athena-given strength—a power that, if Damien's reaction in the bar was any indication, could clearly drive straight behind a vampire's formidable defenses with little effort.

"You're sure his life is in danger?"

"His existence, yep. The star card flipped over for Damien," I responded.

Rex leaned back on his bar stool. "Well, if someone killed him, that would cause a problem for the vampires in Central Florida." He frowned. "That would cause a huge problem, actually."

I ignored that statement for the moment but noted it. "He claimed he partially owned this place," I said. "Does he?"

Rex looked like he wanted to lie, but he shook his head. "No. No, he doesn't. However, his close friend, Killian Jarrow, does own a stake in the club. Since they live in the same vampire nest, Damien sees Sanguine as his, too." Rex frowned.

"It's a joint venture with Killian that's, hopefully, about to come to an end."

"So, you and Killian own Sanguine. But you're not happy with the partnership." Rex's voice was neutral, but I sensed actual distaste for the man. "Why?"

"Vampires can be… what's a polite word? They can be vindictive," Rex said. "Killian isn't a nice guy, even by vampire standards. He's one of the few who actually enjoys all the aspects of being a vampire, and he has no shame in using his powers to keep people in check. I don't particularly like being one of those people. Or around those people." Emma's brother glanced toward Damien. "Damien's a little better than Killian, but not by much." The vampire cleared his throat, looking uncomfortable. "Still, Damien's decapitation would be a problem."

Traditional methods of killing vampires include decapitation and stuffing the severed head's mouth with garlic; a sacred (blessed though not silver) bullet; a stake through the chest (not necessarily through the heart), and so on. Some of these may work on some vampires and not others, and it was hard to tell what would work from vampire to vampire.

Like witches' powers, vampire powers varied.

Some vampires are supposed to be able to transform into bats or wolves, whereas others can't. Some are said not to cast a reflection, while others do. Holy water is said to repel or kill vampires, while others might take a bubble bath in it for the irony.

Because of the variance, a vampire would be hard to protect.

I suddenly remembered reading somewhere that carrying a small bag of salt with you is the best way to stop a vampire. If you are being pursued, you have only to spill the salt on the ground behind you. The vampire must stop and count every grain before continuing the pursuit.

I eyed the salt shaker on the bar and thought about tossing some at Damien, but I refrained.

"So, tell me about Damien," I said simply, my will pushing toward Rex like a gentle breeze. I wanted him to answer.

He pressed his lips together. "Why?" I ignored the question, waiting for the magic Archie claimed I possessed to compel Rex. "Fine," he finally said. "Damien was once the leader of a vampire nest near Atlanta, but he was cast out for some reason. I'm not sure what. He was seen as a Kennedy-like candidate, groomed for greatness, with a beautiful girlfriend, Adriana, at his side."

I blinked. "Wait. Are you saying Kennedy was a vampire?"

Rex stared at me but didn't respond.

"Okay, I get it." I nodded. "Back to Damien. Ruthless, is he?"

He shook his head. "No. Just…not wise. Impulsive. He's been a little more involved with the human world than others, which has pissed off some more traditional vampires. But, of course," Rex smiled, "you could say the same of me. It's also raised his profile in the vampire world, as well." He gave me a sidelong look. "Being Killian's best friend probably doesn't hurt, either."

"Why's that?"

"Killian's known for being a bit of a bully. He's also the Ambrogio representative here in Central Florida. Hence his co-ownership of this club with me."

The Ambrogio was the worldwide government that ruled over vampires. The Witches' Council used to treat them with disdain, dismissing their claim of governance and rolling their eyes at any insistence of independence from the rest of the paranormal world. Since the collapse of the Witches' Council rule, I'd heard the Ambrogio had a single representative in the newly elected government. Still, they'd thus far chosen to maintain their parallel shadow government.

"Ah. Yeah, killing a guy nesting with the Ambrogio rep might cause problems here." I looked at Damien, who was, at the moment, no more than a few feet away from us, sneering. "If Killian's more of a bully than Damien? I'd hate to be the puppy that walked in front of the guy. The dude's really unpleasant."

He looked at Damien. "Yeah. I'm not saying Damien's a good guy. But I think he'd prefer to run away from trouble versus running toward it. I can't say the same about his buddy Killian."

I leaned forward, still pushing gently with my will—surprised that Rex didn't seem to notice. "You mentioned he—Damien—was banished from his previous group. Do you know why he was kicked out of his vampire nest in Atlanta?"

Rex shrugged. "Some kind of power play, I think. I'm not really sure. I don't know that much about the back room politics of the Atlanta vampire world."

"Why would Damien's murder cause a major problem in Central Florida?" I asked, curious. "Any other reason than his proximity to Killian?"

Rex shook his head. "It wouldn't in itself. But

Killian Jarrow might turn it into an issue. Especially after the thing that happened between the two of them."

"What thing?" I asked, pushing slightly stronger, hoping to learn more.

He rubbed his face. "I…I don't really want to get into it."

Rex Sullivan didn't notice my will pushing against his defenses, and no one else in the club did either—well, except Archie, who kept a wary eye on things. But no matter how hard I pressed him, he refused to say more.

I guess I wasn't infallible.

Bummer.

"One last question," I asked Rex, my eyes narrowing. "If you heard that Damien Elkhart had been murdered, what's the first name that would pop into your head concerning that crime?"

"Killian Jarrow," he responded without hesitation.

"Thanks," I said, giving him a quick smile. I was sure my face had been impassive, but I caught Damien eyeing me with interest and suspicion as I turned to leave. "One more one last question. Is he here tonight?"

"Jarrow?" He shrugged. "I think he's in

Orlando right now. But he's scheduled to be back on Friday."

"Thanks for the info. Can you excuse me for a minute?" I looked around. "I want to make sure my sister's okay."

He nodded. "Come find me before you go," he said.

I walked toward the front and saw Damien speaking animatedly with a woman on a staircase leading to the bathrooms. I barely had time to register I recognized her before she drew a gun.

I RUSHED FORWARD as the gun fired, Archie's talons digging mercilessly into my shoulder to hang on. My ears were ringing, and I could barely hear the thumping music. Then, with my first racing step, I threw out a sustained vision of a magical shield around Damien—not knowing whether it would work or not.

Damien's head jerked from the bullet's impact before he fell backward on the stairs, and I cursed. The star card had glowed *not even a half an hour ago,* and the vampire I was supposed to save was flopping down the wide club stars like a rag doll.

"Gun!" someone screamed.

"Get out!"

"Run!"

Chaos was erupting. Panic was building. This was Florida, and a gunshot in a club was no joke. The bouncer guarding the entrance stepped back, a look of shock on his face as hundreds of people ran toward him at once.

"Ow," Damien complained loudly as he rolled over and looked down at his chest. "That was quite painful."

I scanned quickly, relieved there wasn't a mark on him.

I barely registered that the woman had dropped the gun. She was now reaching down for a stake in the side of her boot. I launched over the vampire and raced up the stairs just as she raised the wooden stake above her head and fixed her eyes on the still moving and existing Damien Elkhart.

"You will not kill him," I said forcefully, shoving my will at her with all my might. "Put the stake down, and step back before every vampire in the place rips you limb from limb."

Her eyes widened at the power in my voice. "Why the hell not?" she snapped. "I'm a vampire hunter, and he's a vampire! You have vampires in this town!"

"Because he's not the only one, and you will be killed if you do." I gestured toward the dance floor, now eerily silent but still bathed in multicolored lights. Echos of screams from the front of the house provided a final creepy soundtrack. "They will kill you, and you know it. You'll never make it out of here alive."

I grabbed the woman's wrist and yanked the stake away, throwing her over one shoulder to Archie's angry protestive squawking on the other. I winced as I heard her head hit the wall behind me. "Sorry!" I took the stairs down two at a time toward Damien and tucked the stake into the back of my jeans, cursing every person I knew for giving me the crap they had about wearing my uniform in public.

I grabbed Damien by his arm and yanked him to his feet.

"Stand up," I hissed at Damien, who was staring at me as if I'd lost my mind. "You're okay. I shielded you. We have to get out of here. Now."

As the humans crushed through the exit door in fear and panic, the number of vampires in the club—staring at the vampire hunter with an unmoving intensity—became apparent. It wasn't as many as you would think for a club owned by two vampires, but it was more than I wanted to defend the woman against.

I looked at the exit. Unless I could suddenly fly, there was no way to get through the crush of people—and if the vampires went after her and we were in that crowd, others could be hurt.

Damien looked around, his cold body slumped against me, as if he suddenly realized what was going on. "Oh," he gasped, his eyes wide and his voice breathless. "Oh, wow. I should…I should thank you. I should…"

"Damien," I snapped. "Just shut up and stand up. Please." I looked up and found Rex's shocked face. "Where's the room?"

Rex opened his mouth, closed it, and opened it again, like a fish being dragged from the safety of the water.

"Rex! I know you have a secure vampire room! Now, where is it?"

He snapped his mouth closed and pointed toward a nearly invisible door on the other side of the room. "Through there." The club owner paused for a moment, looked around, and then headed toward the door he'd just pointed out so quickly my eye couldn't follow the movement. "You'll be safe in here."

I grabbed Damien's arm and pulled him along, practically dragging him in my haste. As we made it to the tiny room, I heard a low, threatening whisper. "You have to come out with that vampire hunter at some point, witch."

"Sunlight, Dracula," I snapped as Rex slammed the door behind us. "Comes every day like clockwork."

CHAPTER THREE

*R*ex sighed and leaned against the closed door, his weight pressing against it. As I shoved the vampire hunter against the wall (across the small room from the vampire she'd attempted to kill), Rex said, "Do you really think it was a good idea to bring Damien and the woman that tried to murder him in here together and then lock the door? This room isn't all that big, Astra."

"I can only deal with one thing at a time," I responded.

"Yeah, but—"

"If I left Farah Featherbrain out there with your vampire buddies, she'd be a midnight snack for one, two, or all of them," I explained. Then, turning to the woman, I asked, "What's your deal anyway? Are you suicidal or just drunk? You realize you just walked into a vampire-owned bar and went after one of their own, don't you?" She stared at me coldly. "I knew vampire hunters were reckless, but I didn't know they were stupid."

"How did you know my name?"

"Your name really is Farah Featherbrain?" Damien asked, his head tilting to the side. "Did your parents despise you when you were born?"

Farah's dark eyes blazed with hatred. "My first name is Farah, moron," the woman answered, grinding her teeth. She glanced at me and looked confused, then a look of surprised recognition flashed across her face. "Wait a minute." Her eyes narrowed. "I know you."

"Yep," I agreed. "I'm Astra. Nice to make your acquaintance. And you are Farah Hutter, annoying human and Buffy Summers wanna-be."

"She's a chosen one?" Rex said skeptically, his eyes narrowing as he studied the pale woman in front of us. "I find that even harder to believe than her parents not disliking her from the moment she popped out."

"You're a really disagreeable vampire, you know that?" I asked Damien.

Farah's jaw dropped. "Wait. There really are chosen ones?"

"Oh, now you've done it," Archie muttered, glaring at Rex.

"She's just a run of the mill human with an overdeveloped sense of fiction-inspired adventure," I explained. "And—clearly—an underdeveloped sense of judgment. Unfortunately, this isn't the first time I've run into her. The Witches' Council had to intercede to fix her screw-ups a few times."

Farah glared daggers at me. "I had those situations completely under control."

"Not surprised you think that considering your arrogant sense of self-worth and inflated fantasy book sense of purpose," I told her. "But you didn't have those situations under control. And you can't just run around killing people. Not even vampires."

Her expression was grimly determined. "Your Council collapsed, didn't it? So, who's going to stop me?"

I gave her a scathing, exasperated look. "Just about everyone eventually if you're stupid enough to go around killing paranormals. But if you're stupid enough to go around killing vampires in a vampire bar with the vampires themselves on hand to stop you, the answer is likely the six vampires waiting for you to come out of this room."

Farah stared at me for a long moment and then said, "Look, I'll find him and destroy him wherever you might try to hide him, so you might as well save me the trouble and let me kill him now."

Archie snorted. "Oh, for goodness' sake. Did you hit your head today?"

The vampire hunter didn't even glance at the owl. At least there was one person paranormal adjacent that couldn't hear Archie's snaky opinions on this evening's drama.

Rex moved to stand next to me. "So, you know her?" he asked.

"I do," I replied, turning back to face Damien. "Well, I know of her, anyway. After that ridiculous Joss Whedon show came out, many teen girls decided it was up to them to kill vampires. A few got so out of hand we had to intervene." I pointed. "Farah was one of those."

"It was not a ridiculous show," she responded haughtily.

"Let us out of here, and I'll kill her for you," Damien offered with a smile.

This room held far too much murderous intent for my liking.

"I brought her in here so the vampires outside wouldn't kill her, and she wouldn't kill you," I said with a glare. "So, no." I looked at Rex. "Your doormen couldn't tell she was a vampire slayer when she walked in here?" I asked, surprised.

"Stop calling me a vampire slayer!" Farah snapped.

We turned and stared.

"Look, I know what I said before, but I'm not a vampire slayer. I didn't start doing this because I watched some show on television, and I'm not a teenager." She crossed her arms. "I know you witches think you're better than just about everyone on the planet, but stop denigrating me like I'm someone to be dismissed. I got in here, and I almost got a bullet in him." Farah jerked her chin toward Damien. "I would have succeeded in killing him if it wasn't for you and your stupid magic."

"As I said. Let me out of here, and I'll kill her for you," Damien said again.

Despite the sarcastic banter, it was easy to tell from the way people and paranormals were holding themselves that everyone in the room had serious intentions. This room could erupt into violence at any moment. "Could you try and shut up for five minutes? Please?"

Damien gritted his teeth in annoyance and held out a hand, palm up.

"If you're not a vampire slayer, what are you?" Rex asked.

"I'm a vampire retributionist. I don't go around randomly killing vampires. I don't want all vampires to be killed. I'm hired by towns or families that know about vampires and are being menaced by them. Or by people wanting revenge for a vamp that screwed them over," she said, glaring at Damien. "You should have stayed out of Cassandra, buddy. You and your friend Killian turned the wrong party girl against her will."

DAMIEN RELATED the story to us without an ounce of guilt or a flicker of emotion. There was something so strange and sinister about him now, even more than expected for a vampire—he clearly had not a single drop of remorse.

He and his friend Killian visited Cassandra on Halloween and "fell in" (his words) with a group of college students either too drunk to realize they were predators or too stupid to stay sober enough to keep their wits about them. One of the young ladies of the group was Ivy Masterson, the daughter of a Cassandra psychic.

"One thing led to another, and…well, we didn't intend to turn her," Damien shrugged. "It just happened."

"That's not something that just happens," Rex told Damien.

Damien shrugged.

"And then you left," Farah seethed. "Leaving her alone to go through it before she even knew what was happening."

"She was in her mother's house at the time," Damien pointed out blandly. "We figured her mother would take care of her. Cassandra's a town full of people quite aware of the paranormal. So she was in good hands. For goodness' sake, we didn't leave her on the church's steps right before sunrise."

We all stared at him, shocked.

"What? Like I said. It was an accident." He looked around at all of us. "The girl wasn't our responsibility."

"A young woman is wandering around somewhere, being a vampire and not knowing the first thing about being a vampire," I pointed out. "That you turned. That's not your problem?"

"We didn't kill her, witch," Damien replied with a shrug. "She's still around doing her thing, I'm sure."

Farah gave Damien a nasty look. "She's spending days in a blacked-out room and her nights crying that life as she knows it is over, you useless leech," Farah responded with venom. "She was a person. You're not supposed to just turn someone and leave them," Farah added. "That's evil."

"It's not evil. It's practical. It was an accident. Again, Cassandra's a town full of people aware of the paranormal. Her mother would have dealt with it. Probably did deal with it," Damien said with lackluster interest. "It wasn't our problem."

"Well, it's your problem now," Farah flung back at him.

"What do the town leaders have to say about it?" I asked Farah, stepping in front of Damien before she went for him again.

My boyfriend, Jason Bishop, was the son of the Cassandra mayor. Not only that, the mayor was dating my boss, Captain Harmon of the Forkbridge Police Department. Halloween was months ago—I found it hard to believe I was only hearing about this issue now.

"They don't know."

I blinked. "They don't know? The mayor doesn't know?"

"Ivy is hoping that if she doesn't drink any blood, she'll turn back into a human being, and then nobody has to know what happened to her. You know, like in the Dracula movie?" Farah looked at me. "Everyone in town thinks she's back at college."

"But the ghosts have to know."

"They're keeping her secret." Farah's expression looked pained at the mention of the ghosts. "The longer this went on, however, the more enraged they became." She turned her gaze to Damien and narrowed her eyes. "They came to find me, and they told Mrs. Masterson how to contact me."

To be fair, if I'd heard this story in any other situation, I would have stepped aside and let Farah stake Damien Elkhart right through the heart and then helped the woman clean up any evidence of the retribution. What Damien and Killian did to Ivy was utterly irresponsible for paranormals in general, not to mention unbelievably cruel. Turning someone against their will and leaving them alone to deal with their newfound reality…

It sickened me.

I wasn't supposed to be as bloodthirsty as the Witches' Council, but their death penalty punishments weren't always arbitrary. Execution was sometimes meted out to genuinely evil people, and it was well deserved.

I pulled out the star card.

It was still glowing.

I looked at Damien. "I really don't want to keep her from killing you," I admitted. "I've heard many things in my time with the Ministry, but this story really takes the cake. You're a psychopath."

"Rest assured, I'd rather she didn't," Damien told me.

I looked at him and cleared my throat. "I hate to tell you this, buddy, but I'm betting no one in this safe room cares what your preference is."

"You'll step aside?" Farah asked.

I really, really wanted to say yes.

Instead, I held up the glowing star card. I explained to Farah what I'd already told Damien —that the card glowed in the direction of someone whose life was threatened, someone the goddess Athena expected me to keep alive for some reason she never bothered to explain. "So, I have to keep him alive," I told her. "I don't know why she doesn't want him killed, but in the past, Athena's always had fairly good reasons."

"I'm going to kill him," Farah shot back. "You, Astra, did nothing to me, so I won't hurt you just to get at him. And I respect the gods, so I will stay my hand until that card's light goes out." She furrowed her brow. "But only until that card goes out, do you understand? I expect you to get out of my way as soon as your goddess releases her protection on that bloodsucking bottom feeder." She glanced at Rex. "No offense."

"None taken."

I glanced at Damien. "As soon as the star card goes out, she'll be on you like a church mouse on communion wafers," I said.

"I'd really prefer she didn't," Damien said again in a monotone so disinterested it was as if he was stating a preference for it not to rain in two weeks.

"You're really not even sorry, are you?" Farah asked him.

"About Ivy? What good would that do? She's still out there. She's still a vampire. She lives." Damien shrugged. "I'm sorry, but we did nothing wrong here. Not by any standards."

My initial reaction was that he couldn't possibly believe that. And my second thought was that if he did, he was a psychopath who needed to be dealt with.

I glanced at Rex. Vampire though he was, even he looked appalled.

I looked back at the retributionist.

Farah would kill Damien. She couldn't help herself; I could see it in her eyes. It wasn't just what he'd done to Ivy. It was that he felt no remorse for what he and Killian had done to her, what they had taken from her, and the pain they had caused her. That lack of remorse meant he was likely to do it again.

And Farah would not let that happen.

* * *

REX AND DAMIEN telepathically tracked the vampires in the club as they lost interest in Farah one by one. A bang on the door echoed through the small metal-lined room when there were only two left. "Astra? Rex?" Emma shouted. "Are you guys in there?"

Rex frowned. "She just can't stay out of these things, can she?"

"Have you met your sister?" Archie responded.

Emma was covering for the evening supervisor that day, so she must have heard the call for shots at Rex's club and come to check it out with the officers.

Rex flung open the door for his sister.

"Hey," she said as she stepped inside and then looked around. "What's going on? We got a report of shots fired, but everyone left out there said nothing happened—including the people who called us—and they don't know why they're milling around in the parking lot." She pulled out her pad and pen, poised to take notes. "What fresh magical hell have we gotten ourselves into now, ladies and gentlemen?"

"If no one can tell you what happened, the vampires must have glamoured everyone," Rex told her with relief. "So, officially? Nothing happened. We had a fundraiser, it was a great success, and everyone went home. You can put away your notepad. The speaker must have crackled, and someone thought it was a gun."

"Uh-huh." Emma looked at her brother and cocked a dubious eyebrow. "You're lucky you were turned into a vampire, not a small wooden boy."

"Unofficially, that vampire hunter tried to kill Damien!" one vamp still milling about called from behind Emma. "Come on, cop, your brother's a vampire! Shoot her!"

Emma glanced over her shoulder and raised her eyebrow again.

"Well. I mean. If you want to," he added somewhat sheepishly.

"How about we all step into the larger room and have a chat, shall we?"

As we all moved into the larger room, Emma looked at me like she was trying to figure out what I was up to. Instead of responding to the unspoken question, I turned to the two vampires waiting. "Did you and your friends just glamour everyone in the bar and parking lot?" I asked them (watching them fidget uncomfortably when I asked the question), "Including my sister and my boyfriend?"

"Um…"

Rex looked at them. "You glamoured the witch and the…Jason?"

The female vampire shrugged. "It's what we do in situations like this."

"I'll go find them," Archie muttered and launched off my shoulder toward the entrance. "Stupid vampires. Glamouring hundreds of civilians like they're on an episode of…" His voice faded as he went out the door.

Emma crossed her arms over her chest. "Okay, what were you guys doing in the safe room, and why did you try to kill Damien?" she asked. "And why does she have a gun?" she added, pointing at me but looking at Farah. "You can't bring a gun in here. Under Florida Law, a person cannot carry firearms inside an establishment whose main purpose is to sell alcohol."

"I follow a different set of requirements," Farah told Emma.

"Is there a single paranormal group that follows the laws of the place they live? Like, just one?"

"She's not paranormal," I told Emma.

"What is she then?" Emma turned and asked. "A demon?"

"No," I told her. "She's a vampire retributionist."

"Uh-huh." The detective paused. "Yeah, no idea. Which is what exactly?"

"She's a sort of vampire executioner," I told her. "It is her job to take out dangerous vampires, often when they've gone rogue."

Emma's eyes narrowed. "Who gave her that job?"

"I gave me that job," Farah answered proudly.

"She is a killer." Again, Damien's tone was sharp.

"Well, pot and kettle and all that, right?"

Emma said with an amused expression. "Is she staying in town?"

I shrugged. "She's here because she was trying to take out Damien."

"He's still standing there."

"I stopped her."

Emma's expression didn't change. "Why?"

I reached into my jeans pocket and pulled out the glowing star card.

"For him?" Emma asked, incredulous, pointing toward Damien. "But he's a vampire. Isn't he already dead?"

"Not dead enough," Farah said, stepping forward. "I can change that."

Emma's eyes widened for a moment. "So, she's here to kill him because…"

We quickly went through the story.

The two vampires in the large room looked at Damien with undisguised disgust as we related the tale. Then, finally, the female vampire turned away from him with an angry snarl after we were finished. "You have no more quarrel from me, vampire retributionist," she growled. "He is irredeemable."

"Well, wait, Vivaria," the male vampire said, looking concerned. "He made a mistake, but we don't know the whole story. Killian was there, and so there must have been a reason—"

"Shut up, Milka," she snapped.

He chased after her, and in seconds, they were both gone.

"Boy, you're making friends all over the place," Emma observed. "I can't say I'm surprised. But, on the other hand, I want to shoot you myself after hearing that story."

"I didn't do anything wrong!" Damien became enraged and protested. The vampire's only emotion seemed to be indignation that anyone wanted to hold him accountable for anything. I couldn't figure out why the goddess Athena would want this horrible excuse for a paranormal to live.

Emma looked at him for a long moment. "If I had a dollar for every time I heard that from someone victimizing someone else, I swear, I'd be rich," she said. Then, looking back at Farah, she went on. "You say you're a vampire retributionist, and I get why you're doing what you're doing, but how is that going to square with what Astra has to do?"

"I will allow him to exist until that card goes out and the witch has done what she has to do for her gods," Farah said. "After that? All oaths are off."

Emma glanced at her, and then at Damien, and then nodded. "Seems fair."

Archie flew in. "I found them. You probably want to come with me."

"Why?" I asked, wincing as his talons dug into my shoulder again. "Are they okay? Why didn't you bring them in with you?"

"They're fine," the owl told me cheerfully. "They're just standing with the body."

"What body?"

The body was behind the club near the dumpsters.

And the body's name?

Killian Jarrow.

CHAPTER FOUR

"*D*amn," Rex muttered.

We were all standing in the alley behind the club, staring down at the body.

"Yep. He's dead." Emma took out a Maglite, turned it on, knelt, and shone it on the body, pausing for a few seconds on the elaborate knife protruding from Killian's chest. She straightened up after a few moments, a puzzled expression on her face. "Well, I'll be damned. An actual human murder." She frowned. "That's going to be a lot of paperwork."

"No, it's not. He's not human," Rex told his sister. "That's Killian Jarrow. He's a vampire." He frowned. "But I don't know why he didn't alert us. He should have."

Emma looked up. "Hold up. This is the vampire that was with this other idiot in Cassandra when Ivy was turned? That Killian Jarrow?"

"Just to further complicate things, he was the Ambrogio representative here in Central Florida," I told her.

"And co-owner of Rex's club for some reason," Archie added.

Emma looked around with surprise. "Wait, what? He owns the club?"

"It's…complicated," Rex answered.

"Oh, please. It's not complicated at all," Damien said with a dismissive wave. "Rex's club Sanguine has been designated as Central Florida's official Ambrogio safe house. This necessitates adhering to a number of Ambrogio rules, one of which is that the Ambrogio representative must be a co-owner in order to ensure the location's safety and continuity."

"You keep mentioning these rules and regulations," I said to Damien, my head tilted. "Do you guys have rules about not turning people into vampires against their will? Or did you deliberately skip any rules that protect the human population?"

"Well, of course, we're not supposed to." Damien nodded. "Clearly, vampire class structure ensures inherent benefits for the representative. And those around him," he answered with no shame.

"Did he say what I just think he said?" Ami whispered appalled.

"If you require my assistance in dumbing it down? Power comes with a slew of advantages. Killian devoted considerable effort to establishing, developing, and sustaining a power base in the Ambrogio. Naturally, that benefited our nest."

"Not enough," Ami pointed out. "He's dead."

"Good riddance," Farah said with a tempestuous resentment.

Everyone knew that the powerful took advantage of their positions. I mean, it's not exactly a secret. It was a rare person that didn't, even if just a little, if they found themselves in that position. But to actually see someone brag about maxing out that privilege with no shame, right in front of your eyes?

Well, it was something else altogether.

Jason, who'd been silent until now, stared at

the vampire shrugging off the death of his friend. "You seem completely unaffected by his death," Jason said, his voice betraying a fascination with Damien's cold, impassive demeanor. "Don't you have any feelings for him at all?"

"What, should I be sad that I lost him?" Damien raised an eyebrow.

"Um." Jason shifted uncomfortably. "Yes?"

"If you must know, yes, I'm sad that I lost him," Damien responded, his tone devoid of sadness. He peered down his nose at the man lying on the ground with a frosty gaze. "Our nest will almost certainly be smaller than it was previously. Some will depart now that we will have to re-socialize to regain position." He looked up at Jason. "Attaining privileged elevation without a Ambrogio representative is not easy."

Damien went on to explain how his friend Killian's death would be difficult for everyone who rode on the dead vampire's powerful coattails, but I stopped listening. I didn't care what he had to say anymore. In fact, I wasn't sure I wanted to speak with him again for any reason if I could help it.

The vampire was heartless. Heartless, indifferent, unemotional, callous.

I'd met a lot of paranormal creatures while

working for the Ministry, but I'd met no one as coldly aloof and unfeeling as Damien Elkhart. The iciness made it difficult to read him, but one thing I marked about him. Since we walked out to look down at Killian Jarrow's body?

Damien Elkhart never ever seemed surprised.

Maybe it was because Killian was Damien's partner in crime, and the other vampire's death coming so soon after an attempt on his own life didn't surprise him in the least. Perhaps it was because he was so self-absorbed that he really didn't care about anyone but himself. It's possible that the lack of surprise was understandable.

Or maybe there was more going on here than met the eye.

Damien looked at me sharply as if he picked up on my thoughts.

I raised my eyebrow. "Question?"

He shook his head. "For you? Not likely."

I turned toward Emma's brother. "What did you mean when you said you didn't know why he didn't notify you, Rex?" I asked Emma's brother. "Him as in the dead guy?"

Rex nodded. "When vampires die, other vampires feel it and sense it for miles around. We come quickly to remove the body and cremate it so no autopsy can be done and no one can examine it," he explained. Rex looked down at Killian once more, a pained expression on his face. "I didn't sense his death at all. Not even a whisper."

I turned to Farah. "So, I have to ask. Not that I would blame you," I added sympathetically. "But did you kill this vampire?"

"Killian didn't turn Ivy. Damien did," Farah said. She turned her head slightly and met his cold stare with a fiery gaze. "Killian let him get away with it and abandoned her, too, even though Damien's turning and leaving violated the Ambrogio's rules. So, yes, maybe he deserved some retribution, too." She looked me in the eye. "But no. I would claim this death proudly if I had a hand in it. But I didn't."

I put on my gloves, reached forward and pulled the knife from Killian's chest with one swift move.

"Ugh! Astra! You really had to do that?" Ami asked, horrified.

"I did," I told her, holding up the knife and scrutinizing it. There, in tiny letters, was what I was looking for: Property of the Ministry etched carefully on the bevel. "It's a Ministry blade. If I had to guess, it's ensorcelled somehow to ensure that whatever magical death call you vampires give out is blocked."

* * *

VAMPIRES SWARMED from all directions within moments of the vampire death blade's removal. I wasn't sure where they would take the body, but I was relieved to see that many vamps who showed up expressed sorrow over Killian Jarrow's death. It reminded me that vampires as a species weren't the evil here.

Damien, however, said nothing.

And he didn't lift a single finger to help.

"You wanna tell me what we need to do here?" Emma asked as she, Farah, Ami, and I stepped away from the vampire body moving squad. "Because I find it hard to believe Damien Elkhart is really the pivotal piece of this puzzle."

Ami raised her eyebrow. "The police don't have any need to investigate Killian Jarrow's murder, do they? He wasn't human. You don't have a case."

"The captain and I have talked a few times about this, and while technically that vampire's death isn't a police issue," Emma admitted, leaning against the wall of the club and crossing her arms, "we need to deal with it. He and I both believe that because we know our town is crawling with paranormal creepy crawlies, it's best to stay informed about what they're up to."

"Did you just call me a creepy crawly?" Archie asked, his feathers fluffed up indignantly.

"No, not you," Emma told him as she raised an eyebrow at him. "You're too cute to be creepy. And I don't mean that in an insulting way. I really don't. It's just that—"

Rex popped up in the middle of our circle as if out of thin air.

"The story," he responded, "is that Damien Elkhart is biding his time, waiting for his opportunity to make a bid for the top spot in the Ambrogio for Central Florida. Killian Jarrow was his biggest obstacle, and now that someone's taken care of him, he'll make his move." He looked at me. "Just a rumor that came with the body brigade. I don't know how true it is, but they believe it."

In another blink, he was gone.

"I hate that fast-as-lightning vampire crap," Emma muttered, gazing after him.

Farah reached into her pocket and handed Emma a lavender pouch. "Here," she said, holding it out. "Take a pinch of this and throw it on him.

He won't be able to use his speed for about five minutes or so."

The detective's eyes widened. "Are you serious?"

"As serious as a poltergeist," the vampire retributionist responded.

Emma accepted the gift and nodded a thank you. "Oh, I can't wait to use this. Got anything else in that pouch that will shut him up?"

Farah chuckled but didn't volunteer another pouch.

"Let's refocus, ladies." I pulled out the star card. "The card is still glowing. Unless Farah's lying to me and is planning to make a move on Damien before the card says I'm off the clock—"

"I'm not."

"—she's not the threat to Damien's life," I continued. "Do you think there's another retributionist on the case? Is it possible Ivy or her family hired someone else to go after Killian while you were hired to go after Damien?"

Farah shook her head emphatically. "Never. We coordinate. We'd have to for our own safety, right? If there was another retributionist stomping around Forkbridge, I'd know about it."

"Are you sure?" Emma asked her.

"We have a group text, so I know where everyone is."

Ami put a hand on my arm. "Astra, don't forget about the reading I did for Damien. He may not seem to care about much, but whoever the woman was in the reading? He cares about her. Judging from what he's said, she may be the only other thing he cares about besides power."

"That was his ex, right?"

"It sounded like." Ami looked up, her face tense. "I don't think he said her name."

"I wonder if it's the Adriana person Rex was telling me about," I said, turning to glance at the vampires and Jason wrapping Killian in a shroud. "Rex said Damien was the leader of a nest in Atlanta, but he got kicked out for some reason."

"Some reason?" Farah chuckled. "He got kicked out by Killian Jarrow."

We all turned and stared at her, surprise on our faces.

"Well, I don't just race across the country with a stake in my hand and leap out from the bushes, you know," she said, her expression tight. "I did quite a bit of homework on Damien before I decided to make my move, so I know a lot about him." She turned. "I'd be happy to help you out on this glow card thing if you want."

I paused and looked at the young woman. Her problems with the Ministry stemmed from an overdeveloped sense of duty to a path she had chosen but not been chosen for—not something the Witches' Council would care to respect. Even though I felt her heart was in the right place, I wasn't sure I could trust her to follow my lead.

In the end, I gambled. "I'd appreciate that, thanks."

"Absolutely," she nodded. "We'll get to the end of it faster."

"Astra, are you sure you can trust her?" Emma asked, eyeing Farah suspiciously. "She did just try to murder someone in the middle of my brother's club."

"That's what Althea's potions are for," I said, shrugging.

"Come again?" Farah asked, but I ignored her question.

She would either drink Althea's truth potion and willfully submit herself to forced veracity, or she wouldn't. No reason to give the vampire retributionist time to think about whether she should.

"What are you going to do with the vampire?" Archie asked.

"Damien?"

The owl nodded.

"I think we'll need to talk to Rex about using the bunker."

Farah blinked. "The…bunker?"

"Last year, there was this big conspiracy to capture vampires and—well, anyway, Rex owns their bunker now," I told Farah. There was no need to give the human more information than she'd already been able to figure out about paranormals on her own. "It's pretty large, super secure, underground, and has everything we need to be able to come and go during the day while keeping the vampires safe."

"I thought he was going to turn it into a vamp B&B?" Emma asked.

"It is. I did. I mean, sort of. I didn't want to shout it from the rooftops while Killian and the Ambrogio co-owned the property," Rex said, popping back into the conversation. "This town would have been crawling with vampires, and while I like what I am well enough, some vampires are"—he looked at Damien—"something to be concerned about."

"You didn't want to do what while Killian was alive?" Damien asked, sidling up to the group with a sly smile.

Not sure if I mentioned it, but vampires have

incredible senses. Very heightened. They can hear things from great distances. They can also hear things like heartbeats or respirations—which makes them excellent lie detectors.

That Damien didn't hear what we were discussing?

Not likely.

He was either lying about not hearing what we said, was too distracted to pay attention, or was too self-centered to bother with information outside of his own head unless it was about him.

Oh, yeah.

And vampires are telepathic.

"Don't worry about it," Rex told Damien.

Damien's smile faltered. "When I am the Ambrogio representative, you will not be so patronizing about my requests," Damien told Rex, clearly having heard the conversation he asked about. His eyes flickered with self-perceived god-like power. "In fact, I'd like to visit this bunker of yours," he added. "Since—when I am finally an Ambrogio—it will be mine, won't it?"

Damien smiled an innocent smile that somehow was more chilling than the cold, expressionless face he usually wore.

Emma buried her face in her hands. "Oh, brother."

"Whatever," Damien said, his expression switching to one of annoyance. "Let's get on with this safe house thing, shall we? I want this over by the time the Ambrogio shows up to appoint me." He stalked away, heading toward the bunker. "When I am an Ambrogio, I will tear down these things and rebuild this limping, passive society as I see fit."

"Are you sure we can't let Farah kill him?" Emma asked me. "I mean, what's the worst that could happen?"

I didn't know, but if the obnoxious Dictator-wanna-be kept going the way he was, I'd probably be okay with testing the bounds of my own Athena rules to find out.

* * *

REX PLACED his hand on a expensive, advanced biometric lock, and it clicked open. "Come in," he said, opening a metal door thick enough to absorb a nuclear blast. The rich smell of food and drink lingered in the air, mingled with the scent of wood and iron.

The stairway immediately inside the door of the small stand-alone building that served as a sunlight mantrap (or vamp trap) led downstairs to another thick security door and another lock.

"Whoa," I gasped as the door swung open.

The bunker was no longer a dungeon for discarded vampires to wither away in captured solitude. It was now warmly lit and decorated with mahogany furniture and plush leather couches. The floor was polished wood and shining marble.

"Rex, this is incredible," Emma breathed.

The spacious rooms were lined with large art on the patterned walls, and our shoes clicked against the expensive marble flooring. A fireplace burned warmly between two faux windows that displayed the night sky, and imposing columns supported by wrought-iron girders soared upward in a circular arched ceiling.

"When did you do all this?" Ami asked.

"Oh, here and there," he said. "I've rented it out for a few private parties, but I haven't been very public about it."

"To vampires?" I asked.

Rex looked at me but didn't respond.

"It's adequate," Damien said with a condescending roll of his eyes.

Emma stared at him. "Wow. Just…wow."

Damien stared back. "Wow?" he asked, his tone mocking.

"You're literally the most patronizing dude I've ever met," Emma told him with an exasperated finger point. "What the hell is wrong with you? Did they suck out your brain when they made you a vampire? Did you watch Twilight one too many times and think Ari, the smug leader of the Volturi—that's who I want to be when I grow up?" Emma threw her purse down on a side table. "And you needed a tarot reading to determine why a woman left you? I got news for you, buddy; I could have given you a bullet-pointed list—"

The vampire's face contorted into a snarl as he roared with rage and extended his hands toward Emma's throat. In another blink of an eye, he disappeared and reappeared on the other side of the room, just feet in front of the detective, who stood motionless. It seemed like he would close the gap between them in an instant and end her life with ease.

I mean, it *seemed* that way.

"No!" Farah shouted, and she raced toward Emma, desperate to save her from the vampire's vengeance.

The rest of us…didn't.

The retributionist was halfway to the brewing confrontation when the vampire slammed against an invisible barrier wrapped around Emma like a cocoon and lurched clumsily to the floor. Damien struggled on the ground, eyes wide, gasping for air, his fingers clawing at his throat, desperate to pull away from the invisible hands choking him.

Suddenly, he collapsed in a heap, unconscious.

"That was fun to watch," Archie admitted vengefully.

"It really was, wasn't it?" Emma agreed cheerfully. "You think he'll do it again? I think he's going to be one of the ones that just can't believe it. He'll have to prove it to himself. Repeatedly."

"Oh, surely not," Ami said.

Emma gave Ami a mischievous look. "Bet me?"

Farah stood stock still, shocked at what she'd seen. "Wait." She blinked. "What? What just happened? Is there an anti-vampire ghost in here?" Her head swiveled on her neck. "Does Emma have a guardian?"

"Give it a second," I said, pointing toward Damien. "It'll be funnier if you wait."

The waking vampire's face blushed a livid

shade of crimson as he struggled to his feet. "What did you just do to me?" he snarled. He lunged for Emma again and fell to the floor with a harsh thud, stunned. "What is happening?" he howled.

Emma leaned toward him, smiled, and said, "Vampire repellent, baby."

"There is no such thing!"

"Come at me, bro," she responded with a wide smile. "Let's see who's right."

"I'm glad I didn't take that bet," Ami murmured.

"My sister is a potion master," I told Farah as Damien got up, reached for Emma, and fell on the floor choking again, and again, and again. "Last year, Rex and I got into a bit of a disagreement, and she whipped up a potion that activates when a vampire attacks. I'm not sure how it works or why it works, but as you can see —it works."

"That is incredible," Farah breathed, her eyes glued to the vampire.

"Althea's a master at crazy potions. Though this one isn't really a potion. It comes in pill form," I explained. "We all take it every day with our vitamins. Just in case."

Damien finally stood up and angrily walked away from Emma.

"You're all immune to vampire attacks?" Farah asked, astonished.

"All of us. The Ardens, my parents, the captain. Basically, anyone in town that might have issues or run-ins with vampires," Emma told Farah.

Damien brushed off his designer suit before glaring at Rex. "I will kill you for that," he hissed.

"I'd like to see you try," Rex said calmly.

I wanted to see him try, too.

CHAPTER FIVE

The usual tone of one of these gatherings was bleak, concerned, nervous—bleak or concerned or nervous that a death would occur, a crime would happen, a catastrophe would take place we wouldn't be able to stop.

Not this time.

Everyone's dislike of Damien burned so intensely, however, that the light-hearted frivolity I felt as we sat down on the leather couches was absurd and understandable all at the same time.

I couldn't help but take pleasure in the fact that the room's biggest jerk was having a few fits of anxiety—in light, of course, of our impenetrable vampire defenses. Damien was an arrogant, self-absorbed jackass with the demeanor of a sewer rat and the swagger of a bully. If anyone was going to be filled with anxiety and doubt, it *should* be him.

"So, what's the plan for tonight?" Ami asked. She looked at her phone. "Well, what's left of it, anyway."

Emma tried to assert her place as the investigator on the scene.

"There are a few things I'd like to discuss," she said, her professional voice crackling with authority. "Killian's got—or had—a lot of money, a lot of clout, a lot of power. That probably means he had a long list of enemies, so this could take a while. We should probably get a list of those folks and go get statements from them."

"I have a statement," Damien said. "This is a stupid waste of time."

She looked at me. "And does it have anything to do with Damien's star card? That card could be about another attack on his life and not just Farah's."

"You're wrong," Damien said with a smirk, and I wanted to smack it off his face. "Killian had a lot of people who respected him. He was a pillar of the community and a great humanitarian leader—"

"A humanitarian?" I asked, choking on my ginger ale. "Killian Jarrow was a humanitarian?"

"Was he now?" Emma asked in a calm but incredulous voice.

"Yes, a humanitarian. A vampire that still drinks directly from humans," Damien answered with a full-on eye roll. "Anyway, he didn't have any enemies. He had people who hated him and people who feared him."

The rest of us looked at one another.

"So, enemies?" Archie asked sarcastically.

Damien leaned in his chair and stared at Archie with the superior, condescending gaze of a spoiled child who had been scolded for hitting a sibling. "God, you really are utterly annoying, aren't you?"

Farah's head shot up, and she squinted at Archie. "Did that owl just talk?"

Archie bowed extravagantly, his feathers puffed up proudly.

"He just bowed at me. That owl just *bowed*."

"That didn't take long," Jason chuckled.

"What do you mean?" the vampire retributionist asked my boyfriend. When he didn't answer, she turned toward Emma. "What did he mean?"

"We don't know for sure who can hear Archie

and who can't, but what we've hypothesized is that people who believe in the paranormal are more likely to be able to hear him. For those that don't, he's just a regular owl," Emma explained. Emma's eyes swiveled to Damien. "And for those that are supernaturally ethics challenged or rude to him," she said sweetly, "Archie isn't an owl at all. He's a dragon."

Damien's eyes widened, and he scrambled back in his seat.

"Naw, I'm just kidding," she laughed. "He's an owl."

"As far as *you* know," Archie muttered.

"Are we done with the show and tell time and the comedy portion of the evening?" Rex asked his sister impatiently, rubbing his temples. "It's getting on toward midnight, and some of you are going to be falling asleep where you sit. I'd like to come up with a plan before the Ambrogio leaders show up here."

"Ambrogio leaders?" I frowned. "Why would they show up?"

"Their representative *died*, you moron," Damien hissed at me. "They'll be here within hours. You hastened their arrival when you pulled that dampening knife out of Killian's chest like an idiot."

"Dramatic much?" I asked him.

"Much what?" he snapped.

"If that's the case, we need to get through as much information as possible before they arrive here, and we need to come up with our own plan to protect Farah—which might involve sending her back to Arden House for a bit, so we better start talking," Emma said. "Agreed?" She looked around the room. Everyone nodded in agreement except for Damien. "Good."

Damien ran his hand over his face. "This is ridiculous. We need to prepare for the Ambrogio's arrival." Damien's eyes narrowed. "I need to—"

"Damien?" Emma said with a smile.

"Yes?"

"No one asked you."

* * *

"Damien and Killian were both turned by Adriana Kingsley, a three-hundred-year-old female vampire that has a habit of dating men and offering them immortality if they stick around longer than a couple of weeks," Farah said with her arms crossed over her chest. "She's not very choosy. I mean,"—she extended a hand toward Damien—"obviously."

Adriana.

The woman in Ami's reading.

"Even though she's a vampire, she's actually quite harmless. She hasn't had any direct run-ins with the Ambrogio, and she's only ever killed her prey when she was forced to," Damien said defensively.

Well, I mean, as long as she was *forced* to, I thought sarcastically.

"That may be the first time I've ever heard you express a positive feeling toward someone for what seems like no direct benefit to you at all. Why is that?" Emma asked. Damien looked away, shifting in his seat.

When he didn't respond, I told Emma, "He's in love with her."

"I suggest we leave that topic for another time," Damien said immediately. His eyes moved to me and narrowed. "This is none of your business. Any of you." His voice was so intense, so cold.

I pulled out the glowing card. "Here's the thing. This? This says otherwise."

Damien glared at me. His eyes were filled with frustration, and I could see the anger simmering just below the surface.

"I can't say what Damien feels one way or another," Farah began, "if anything. But I can tell you Astra's probably right. Damien and Adriana were together until she left him and turned Killian to be her new vamp boy toy in Atlanta. That's when Damien was kicked out of the Atlanta vampire nest. He didn't take it well."

Rex looked surprised. "You were literally kicked out of your own nest just because Adriana found a new man?" Sympathy flashed on his face as he glanced at Damien—who sneered back with contempt. "That's pretty ruthless. How long had you been a vampire when that happened?"

Damien moved his jaw back and forth a few times. Then he snapped, "I don't want to talk about this! It's the past! It doesn't matter!"

"Two years," Farah told Rex.

"And your reading seemed to indicate that it is still important to you," Ami added quietly. "I don't understand one thing, though—why would you be friends with someone that broke up your relationship and caused you such pain?"

"It wasn't Killian's fault," Damien told her. "It had nothing to do with him. I knew that eventually. And she hurt me because I let her.

Things were different then. I was different then. I've moved on from that! I've—"

"Okay," I interrupted, trying to ignore Damien's anger, which was rolling off him and hitting me in waves. "So, let me see if I understand this. You met Adriana as a human. You got involved with her. Within a few weeks she made you a vampire, and you remained in the Atlanta nest as her partner for the next two years or so—until she met Killian, broke up with you, and repeated the same pattern with him. Is that right?"

Damien's jaw was so clenched that I could almost hear his fangs grinding. It appeared that having what happened laid out so objectively was painful for him. He averted his gaze from me but nodded curtly.

Farah answered, "That's right."

"But how did Killian wind up in Forkbridge?" Ami asked quietly.

Damien laughed—but it was a dark sound that didn't reach his eyes. "Because she obviously did the same thing to him as she did to me. He came to apologize to me."

"Did he?" Rex asked.

"Yes, of course," Damien said, looking at the

table. "Killian and I became friends as a result of our shared suffering. To be honest, I was initially averse to admitting it. I had no desire to be friends with someone who had snatched away something that meant so much to me. However, we became friends, and I discovered that he is actually—" Suddenly, he looked up and pushed himself out of his chair. "No. I'm done discussing this. You tricked me. I don't want to talk about any of this with any of you."

I stood up before he could storm off. "Damien, wait. You said 'that selfish jerk is ruining everything. And it should be me, not him' during the reading." I paused. "Were you talking about Killian?"

Damien's head snapped to me. "What are you talking about?"

"The reading. You implied there was a betrayal, and there was a man involved in whatever this was with you and Adriana. Someone betrayed you. Maybe Killian. Maybe Adriana. Maybe even someone else." I paused. "Who were you talking about?"

Damien's eyes flashed, and I braced for an attack (that would do nothing, anyway.) It didn't come, but Damien's low voice turned even colder. "I'm not discussing this anymore."

"I need to understand what's going on in order to protect you," I said quietly.

"It doesn't matter!" Damien yelled. "It was a joke! It meant nothing!"

"Damien," Rex said, standing up. "It's okay. They only want to help you. They may not like you, but they're serious about protecting you. You can talk about this."

"You moron, that one wants to kill me!" He jabbed a finger at Farah. "Help me? No!"

Emma moved between them, her hands raised out of instinct, as though this were a high school cafeteria and we were about to start a food fight. "Okay, let's calm down."

"Shut up!" He turned abruptly and stormed off toward the far end of the room. "We're done here!" Without waiting for agreement, Damien opened a door leading to another room, stepped through, and stopped to give us all one last dirty look.

"Damien," Emma called after him. "Let us help you."

With dramatic flair, he slammed the door behind him.

"Leave him be," I said. "He needs to calm down."

And I needed to think without the shrieking vampire shouting.

I looked at Emma. "Ami and I both heard him during the reading before any of this happened. He was jealous or resentful of some man, and the man clearly had to do with the woman—and the woman was Adriana." I stared at the closed door and tilted my head. "He spoke freely about Killian here—but as soon as we asked about that man, he clammed up." I looked at Emma. "I don't think it's Killian."

Farah agreed. "Killian and Adriana didn't talk anymore at all, at least as far as I could tell. Damien was right—Adriana unceremoniously kicked Killian to the curb with the same disinterested 'moved on' attitude that she dropped Damien. And when that woman moves on, she moves on."

"What I don't understand is how Killian Jarrow became an Ambrogio rep at such a young age," Rex said, his eyes on the door. "It's impossible. Well, maybe not *impossible*, but it's not like you can just walk into one and say, 'Hi, I'd like to become an Ambrogio.' There's a process, and younger vampires are generally not invited to join. At least the last I heard."

"You were invited," I pointed out.

"No," he argued, "I was not. In fact, that's why Killian had to become co-owner. If this was to be an official safe house, the Ambrogio had to have some level of control over it. They wanted the club and this place on the lair map, but not enough to invite me into the Ambrogio. Killian's fractional ownership was the compromise."

Emma looked confused. "I'm sorry, the *lair map*? What the heck is a lair map?"

Before Rex could answer, Farah told Emma, "It's a global map of vampire-safe sleeping areas, as well as locations where they can obtain food and shelter while traveling. Think of it like Airbnb, only for vampires."

"It's very secret," Rex told her. "Probably our most secret document."

"Yeah, no, it's not. It's on Pirate Bay in a PDF," Farah disagreed. She turned to the detective. "I'll get you a copy, Emma, if you want. It's not too out of date."

Rex frowned at her. "You would."

I looked at Rex. "Could you have told them no? The Ambrogio, I mean. Refused to be on the lair map, refused to give a portion of the club to Killian? Just told them to go pound sand?"

He nodded. "I could have. We have some rights. To be honest, though, I didn't mind. It helps out fellow vampires, and it is the defacto directory for traveling vamps. It wasn't the Ambrogio I had a problem with." His cheeks flushed red with anger. "It was Killian and Damien I couldn't stand."

"So, if it's not Killian in the reading, who was Damien talking about?" I asked.

Emma caught the questioning look on my face, and she tapped her chest with her finger, letting me know she would ask her brother about his problems with the vampire pair later when they were alone. I nodded slightly.

"I also want to know who made Killian a member of the Ambrogio? And why so young?" Ami asked. "Could there be some kind of conspiracy there?"

"And does any of this have to do with Ivy Masterson?" Emma added.

"What I am curious about is why the goddess wants such a wretched vampire protected," Jason, speaking up for the first time in a while, wondered. "There have to be more deserving people walking around."

"And the most important question of all: when are we going to have a midnight snack?" Archie added, his wing pointing toward a clock on the wall. "It's almost one a.m. We've been at this for an hour now, and we're no closer to narrowing anything down at all. In fact, the more you people yammer, the more convoluted this seems to get." The owl hopped along the top of the leather couch with his razor-sharp talons. "I think a snack would help."

"For once, I agree with Archie." Emma looked at the clock and sighed. "I'm glad I'm not the only one who feels like we need a break."

"I think everyone needs to take a step back, take a breath, and look at all of the facts we have." I paused. "We have the star card and the goddess wanting Damien 'alive' for some reason. We have the crime of turning Ivy against her will, which may or may not have anything to do with all this. Killian's been murdered, and Damien's murky history and sparkling personality make *him* a pretty convincing suspect—along with anyone against the Ambrogio and possibly someone from the Ambrogio themselves."

"Then we have Adriana breaking up with Damien *and* Killian, with Damien still pining for Adriana, and some mystery man that Damien resents," Ami added. "Don't forget that—that's when the star card started glowing."

I blew out a long-suffering sigh. "This is an absolute mess."

"Could be a coincidence," Jason said.

"And we could be asking all the wrong questions," Emma said.

"What do we really know about Killian Jarrow? Or Adriana Kingsley?" Ami said, leaning forward. "What did he do before the club? What did she do in Atlanta besides pluck men from the crowd?"

"Well, you'll be able to ask when the Ambrogio investigator gets here," Rex told Ami. She raised her eyebrow. "The Southeast Regional Ambrogio headquarters, or SRA, is in Atlanta."

* * *

WITH VAMPIRE SPEED, Rex had conjured a human buffet out of thin air, complete with cocktail shrimp, sliced meats, nuts, cheeses, and little tiny crackers. He'd even provided Archie a bowl of chicken, beef, and buffalo jerky.

Emma and I sat at the back of the room, eating slowly and chatting softly as our motley crew devoured the charcuterie he had laid out at breakneck speed. "So, what do you think?" Emma asked, her mouth full of French cheese.

"I like the raspberry sauce," I told her, holding up a cracker.

"Not the food," she said with exasperation. "The situation."

I took a bite and chewed it slowly, then swallowed. "I don't know," I finally said. "I know there's something here. I just don't know what it is." I shrugged. "If you want a conclusion now? It's a big, festering pile of garbage."

Emma tilted her head to the side and nodded. "So, what do we do with this information?"

I set my glass on the table beside the couch. "We wait until the Ambrogio gets here. We'll see who they send and how they respond to our questions. That might tell us something, or at least narrow down a direction."

Emma nodded and dug into her food again.

I looked back at Jason and Farah. She was laughing at something he said, her face flushing red. I had no idea what was going on between them, but Jason seemed very interested in whatever it was.

"She's going to be a problem," I murmured quietly, nodding my head toward them. "She's the only one here that's not immune to vampire attacks, so she can't stay here. If she does, Damien might try and take her out. But I'm not comfortable sending her back to Arden House, either. We might need her."

Emma raised an eyebrow. "So, give her the vampire repellent pill?"

I raised my eyebrow. "Do you trust her enough to render your brother defenseless around her?" I asked. "Because that's what that would do. She could cut him to ribbons or stake him through the heart, and he couldn't do a thing to stop her."

Emma looked at Farah, too, who was now actively flirting with Jason. He had the polite grace to look uncomfortable. "No," Emma said. "No, I don't."

"You see my problem."

"I see more than one," Emma muttered, glancing at Farah again.

"One thing I didn't want to say in front of everyone else." I looked at Emma. "That knife that dampened the vampire death call? It would keep the Ambrogio from knowing Killian was murdered." I shifted in my seat. "I—"

With a whoosh and a wave of air, Rex was kneeling beside our table.

"We have a problem," he said. "Derek and Claire sent a message."

I frowned. "Who are Derek and Claire?"

"Some friends of mine in the Ambrogio."

Emma tensed. "What is it?"

Rex's voice was grim. "The Ambrogio has sent us one of their best investigators." He looked around the room. "Rudy Redmond. They know something is going on."

I froze, my blood chilling. My hands clenched on the table.

"Astra, what's wrong? You know him?" Emma asked.

"I know him," I said. My mouth was dry. "I've met him."

I hadn't seen his face in a while, but the name all but sent a chill down my spine.

Rudy Redmond.

If there was one person I did not want coming to Forkbridge, it was him.

CHAPTER SIX

The tension between us was palpable.

"Decanus Arden," the vampire said in a voice as dead as his eyes. "I should have anticipated you would be involved in this debacle somehow." He wore black pants, a black button-down shirt, and a black leather jacket—and looked around the large room with suspicion. "Did I interrupt?" Then he glanced at the buffet laid out. "Celebrating the death of our representative, perhaps?"

"Well, that's offensive," Archie muttered, and he clicked his beak.

"Vampires don't take offense. We take revenge." He looked at the owl. "I know of you," Rudy told Archie.

"Yeah, well, never heard of you, buddy," Archie responded.

A faint smile touched Rudy's blood red lips. He nodded briefly to the others in the room and turned his attention back to me. "I'm a bit surprised to find you so ordinary looking." Dark eyes traveled up and down my jeans, button-down shirt, and black boots. "I'd heard rumors that you left Paranormopolis with a duffel bag full of the Ministry's most deadly tools and still wore your uniform, having turned mercenary."

I remained rooted to my spot. "Yeah, well, you heard wrong."

Although I didn't move, Rudy's slow examination of me propelled Jason forward, and he came to stand slightly behind me. Most of the time, I found his protectiveness cute (though pointless.) With Althea's vampire repellent potion surging through his body, though, his stance wasn't entirely an idle threat—though I doubted Rudy realized it.

"You were one of the most feared fighters in all the Ministry," Rudy said, flicking his attention toward Jason and then back to me. "Yet you rely on him?" he asked, pointing at my boyfriend. "A human?"

"You're assuming I need to rely on someone, Rudolf," I countered, matching Rudy's cold tone. "That's an assumption you might regret if you try to bank on it."

Everyone kept a close eye on Rudy and me. I had no idea what other people thought of him; the vampire's curiosity radiated from him, piercing my mind and pushing all other thoughts out. He persisted in his subtle telepathic probing of my reasons for being here, but I was wary of letting my guard down.

Rudy held himself back from the group, oddly relaxed and confident, sizing up the people around us, mentally sifting through who to trust and who not to turn his back on. "Now you lead an army of normals wearing denim jeans?" Rudy shook his head. "I'm not sure if I should be insulted or impressed. I suppose time will tell."

I didn't know what to say to that.

I didn't care whether he was insulted or impressed.

I wasn't here to prove myself to him or anyone else.

"Just so you are aware, our goddess's oracle warned me that you might be here and that her sister had given you certain…abilities," Rudy explained. "So, don't think you can take me by surprise."

"Wait a minute—*your* goddess?" Emma asked, speaking up for the first time. "Her sister?" He didn't answer. "Who's your goddess?"

One of Rudy's eyebrows rose slightly.

"The Ambrogio follow Artemis," Archie told Emma. "They think all vampires are descended from some dude named Ambrogio that Artemis turned into a bloodsucking super hunter."

"A vampire," Emma guessed.

Archie nodded.

"We don't think. We know we are the greatest of her hunters," Rudy told us proudly. "The children of Ambrogio and Selene were granted many gifts from Artemis. She gave us the power of the bite, of speed, of strength, of heightened senses, of keen vision." He glanced at Damien. "She gave us the ability to make children through our blood." Then he glanced at me. "Much more than the Witches' Council ever gave you."

"Yeah, some blessing," Archie muttered.

"What Rudy neglects to mention is that they were not intended as gifts," I told Emma. "They were curses. Apollo, Artemis, and Hades cursed Ambrogio. Apollo also cursed him with the allergy to sunlight, and Artemis cursed him with an allergy to silver on top of everything else Rudy named." I turned to Rudy. "If you believe the story, anyway."

"Which most people don't," Farah added. "Historians say it's modern vampire propaganda, not some old story handed down from ancient Greece."

"That is, of course, what we want people to think." Rudy said, acknowledging my comment and Farah's words with a brief smile. "We are not like other vampires, Decanus Arden—as you well know. We of the Ambrogio are the only ones who truly deserve to be called vampires."

"Gosh," Emma said, drawing out the word. "That's not arrogant at all."

"It's bull," Archie responded. "Even Artemis claimed it was bull, but she's happy to get followers. Not a lot of virgin warriors running around these days." Archie twisted his head to a ninety-degree angle. "Wonder how your virgin goddess would feel knowing your idiot representative forced a girl to become a hunter against her will."

"She is the goddess of the hunt," Rudy said with a shrug. "All hunters are welcomed by her.

Even you, owl. When you get done serving your uptight—"

"Watch it," Archie hissed, cutting him off. "Artemis is also the protector of maidens, you moron," he continued, his feathery face angry. "She's caused civil wars over less."

Rudy laughed wryly and then frowned. "Enough of this. I did not travel all this way to give a group of small town paranormals a lesson in vampire history." The vampire's expression narrowed slightly. "I don't suppose you will volunteer the name of the vampire slayer?" He tapped one forefinger against his chin, his eyes shrewd as they passed over each one of us. "After all, you came across him and removed the Shroud Blade from his chest. You must have some idea."

My eyes narrowed at Rudy's naming of the blade.

"How did you know that happened?" Jason asked.

"Vampires are telepathic," I told him quietly. "He's reading all of us like a book."

A chill smile briefly touched the vampire's lips. "And how little your friends and family have read of your book, Decanus." Rudy glanced at Ami, who tensed when he said, "Not very adept witches in your family, it seems." The vampire's eyes became suddenly intent. "I would suggest you show more care for those you love"—he turned from Ami back to me—"than the care you showed for those in your charge in the Ministry."

My cheeks flushed with anger. That arrogant, stupid son of a—

"Don't you threaten us, vampire." Jason's voice was hard and sharp as a razor and his fist balled tightly.

"Oh, I wasn't threatening anyone," Rudy said. "You're the one who evokes danger with your stance. The same as she does," he said with a dismissive wave toward me. He looked briefly at Farah and then back at Jason. "You have a fierce protector, Decanus. His mind is—"

"My mind is my own," Jason snapped. "And I'll thank you for leaving whatever's in my mind inside of it. I'm fully capable of speaking for myself."

"And stop calling me Decanus, Rudy," I snapped. "I don't work for the Ministry anymore."

"Ah, but we are always all that we were, are we not?" Rudy countered. "You and I, Astra, will always be that which we are and that which we were. It all lives within us even after we no longer live. The scars, the marks. The memories."

He saluted me with the proper Witches' Council salute, turned, and left the bunker.

As soon as the door closed behind him, the room erupted in questions.

* * *

"OKAY, okay, okay! Stop pelting me with questions! I was Rudy's commanding officer in the military," I said, holding my hand up as I tried to stop the barrage of questions. "He wasn't the most loyal soldier I ever had—he did things his own way and didn't care about following orders if he believed he knew better. But he was good."

"So, wait—he was a witch, and now he's a vampire?" Emma asked. "How does that happen? Or is he a witch and a vampire?"

"He's a vampire," I said simply. "And he's a full vampire, not a witch—he was once the best vampire hunter I knew. He was smart and very powerful." I took a deep breath. "He was also very arrogant and thought the rest of us were beneath him even back then. I doubt that's changed much, judging by what he said."

"What happened to him?" Emma asked. "How did he turn?"

I swallowed hard.

I knew where this was going, and I didn't like revisiting it one bit.

"A little over five years ago, he was on a mission in Egypt," I explained. "Rudy was on the hunt for a vampire who was killing young women. The Ministry had information that this vampire had settled in Cairo, in the home of one of Egypt's wealthy sheiks. He was—" I paused, catching myself. "I sent Rudy to track the vamp down and…and kill him." I glanced at Rex, but his expression didn't change a millimeter. "We're not sure what went wrong, but we know he ran into the vampire. Somehow, the vampire got the better of him and turned him."

Rex looked away.

"And?" Emma asked.

"And what? That's it. That's how he became a vampire."

"Yeah, right. Okay." Emma looked at me, her eyes searching mine. "But there's more than that." Emma's face was concerned. "What happened after that?"

Close friends could be really annoying.

I closed my eyes and took a deep breath in an attempt to clear my mind.

Finally, I opened my eyes and nodded. "I led a group of eight legionaries in the Ninth Cohort. I brought four with me to Egypt to rescue him. It was standard procedure if something like that ever happened." My tongue tingled as if the words were made of acid.

"And?"

I stared at her. "He killed them all and then disappeared. For a while, he was the Witches' Council enemy number one." I glanced at the door. "A year later, he turned up as one of the Ambrogio investigators, and the Council lost its taste for revenge." I frowned. "Probably to avoid a war between Ambrogio and the Council, to be honest."

"The vampires can make soldiers," Jason pointed out quietly, his face pale. "Probably a good choice."

"Not to bring down the mood even further," Archie said finally, "but I don't like the idea of this vamp being on the loose running around in Forkbridge. He betrayed his fellow soldiers. He didn't have to kill them. I don't trust him."

"I didn't trust him before I knew all this," Rex muttered.

"I don't like the idea of him running around Forkbridge, either," I said.

"I'd guess no one likes the idea," Farah said. "But there's nothing we can do at this point. Killing an Ambrogio investigator is only going to bring more of them here. Even I know that much."

"Hey, Lizzie Borden, how about reigning in that blood lust for a second," Archie told Farah sarcastically. "No one said anything about killing anyone."

She rolled her eyes.

"He's not just running around, though, if I'm being honest," I told him. "He's got a purpose. Rudy was an incredibly focused soldier. Bloodthirsty or not, he'll focus on his job. He may not follow all the rules he's supposed to, but he'll get it done."

"The question is whether his job is what he claims," Ami said quietly.

"Well, I didn't say he was honest," I told my sister.

"I think he'll be careful in general," Rex told us.

Emma looked at her brother. "Why?"

"I can't say that I agree with the Ambrogio sect. Any time you take religious belief and twist it up into forced control or government, I find things get dicey." Rex's eyes were fixated on his sister. "They claim we have no souls, that Hades took them when we were turned so we could remain immortal, and I...I don't believe that. I think it gives them license to..." He trailed off. "Anyway, I do have some issues with them. It's true. But they don't like attention, and they have a code," Rex assured us. "Rudy will be discreet in whatever he does."

"But what is he doing?" Farah asked Rex.

The vampire didn't answer.

"And what if he killed Killian?" Emma asked. "That guy showed up here awfully fast. I know vampires are quick, but didn't that seem a little too quick? The man has killed with impunity before." Emma turned to Damien. "Do you think the Ambrogio could have killed Killian?"

He looked appalled at the suggestion. "Of course not. Why would you even ask such a thing?"

"Because Killian had a Ministry blade sticking out of his chest, and Rudy Redmond used to be a vampire hunter with the Ministry," Emma said with grave sincerity. "He knew the *name* of it. There are only two people in Forkbridge that would have a blade like that—"

"That we know of," Rex interrupted.

"Fine, only two that we know of. Astra and Rudy." Emma waved her hand toward me. "And we know Astra didn't kill him. Do you think it was just a coincidence Rudy mentioned the duffel bag full of magical tools you stole?"

"Didn't turn in," I corrected absentmindedly.

"You did say he disappeared on a mission," Farah pointed out. "Would he have had one of those blades on him at the time?"

I shrugged. "It's possible."

Rex looked at Emma steadily. "If he did it, why would the Ambrogio want Killian dead?"

"Well, that's one question, isn't it?" Emma said. "I have about thirty more. Should I start now, or should we write them down?"

* * *

QUESTIONS FLOODED my mind as I sifted through the emotions Rudy's arrival on the scene had brought up in me.

Rudy Redmond had been assigned to the Ninth Cohort after getting kicked out of the palace guard division. Standing around and watching didn't suit his personality, so they sent him off to become a hunter.

Sent him to me.

He had been wild when he arrived. Spoiling for a fight, determined to take on the evil he was sure lurked around every corner. Dedicated to the Witches' Council and its logistic ideal of paranormal life, rigid and uncompromising.

I loved the military itself, but Rudy?

Rudy loved what the military stood for. He was…

He was a zealot. A true believer.

And he's still a zealot, I thought.

He'd believed in the Council and in the power of their ideals. Now? If I had to guess, he was still dedicated to keeping things in line and orderly—his allegiance and ideals had simply changed to follow the Ambrogio.

I'd dealt with a lot of legionaries in my time, and I had a knack for reading soldiers. I could tell the ones who were going to make the best officers and the ones who were going to be a problem.

Rudy was both.

Good, but a problem.

On the one hand, he'd been fearless and focused.

On the other hand, he saw the world in black and white, convinced that he had the right—the duty—to put everything in line. He was, if I was being honest with myself, the kind of zealot I'd once been but had managed to step away from.

Unfortunately, he never could.

"Are you okay?" Archie asked.

I looked down, pulled out of my memories by talons digging into my thigh. "Huh?"

Having flown across the room, my owl had landed on my legs and was peering up at me with concern. "Everyone wisely decided to leave you alone because they figured you needed to work through some things, but *I* more wisely decided you'd had enough of that."

"I'm okay, Archie," I told him, brushing a finger down his soft feathers. "Just thinking about old times."

He hooted softly. "Like what? What are you thinking about?"

"How Rudy would do whatever he needed to in order to serve whatever he believes in," I answered. "And that his change came because I sent him out on a mission that he clearly wasn't well-prepared for." I sighed with profound regret. "He always took it all just one step too far, and eventually, it cost him his eternity—and four legionaries their lives. I lost more than half my Cohort trying to save him."

Archie tilted his head. "It was your job. It was his job. And those legionaries? They knew it was their job, too."

"He would have been one of the best, you know," I said quietly. "Eventually. He might have even gone on to become an officer if he could have just reigned it in a bit. He had that kind of grit, that kind of determination." I sighed. "What a waste."

"Okay, so I have a question."

"Shoot."

"Does what happened in the past have anything to do with what's happening now?"

The owl had a point. A good point, too. "I don't think so."

"Then pull your head out of your denim-encased behind, get up, and get to work. You could arm yourself with some more information," he suggested. "If you learn more about Ambrogio's ideals or plans for Forkbridge, maybe you'll be able to figure out what Rudy's after."

"I hear you, but—"

"Maybe you'll be able to figure out why he's here if his claims aren't on the up and up." The owl leaned forward, resting his head on my hand. "One thing I can tell you. Sitting here moping isn't getting you any closer to letting Farah put a silver bullet between Damien's eyes." His big eyes blinked dramatically. "And isn't that what we all *really* want?"

I chuckled. "Okay, okay," I conceded. "I'm curious, know-it-all. Do you think it was a coincidence Rudy, someone I know, showed up in Forkbridge now?"

"I think it's a sign you need to keep your head in the game," he told me. "And I mean that. I'm not worried about you, Astra. I'm worried about all the people you care about. This thing is too close to Rex, and that means it's close to Emma. That's not even counting the star card and Damien. You're too worried about what's already happened, and that's a mistake. You need to face the current problem, soldier, and not let the past distract you."

"Stop calling me that. I'm not a soldier anymore, Archie," I told him.

"Well, there's one thing you can learn from the crazy witch-turned-vampire," Archie told me, and then he hooted emphatically. "We are always all that we were, and you, goddess-chosen, are still in charge whether you like it or not. So get your head in the game and figure out what's going on in Forkbridge. Don't sulk. And don't look back."

"I don't sulk. I was—"

"Your past is the past. It's the future that's important. And maybe even see if you can convince Farah to stop making eyes at Jason."

"She's not—"

"Oh, yes. She is."

CHAPTER SEVEN

*E*mma and I were sitting in our favorite booth at Joey's Diner the next morning. We'd just finished our breakfast, and our conversation had so far been about minor details rather than the major issues on both of our minds.

I yawned.

"Didn't sleep well, I take it?" Emma inquired as she sipped her coffee. Emma's favorite French Vanilla brew had so much sugar in it that even if she was tired, she wouldn't be after the glucose hit her system.

"I'm awake enough to deal with today. I might need a nap before the vampires come out tonight, though."

When I'd finally dozed off, my dreams were filled with images of legionaries yelling, sand, and the oppressive Egyptian heat. Damien's snide expression and the sound of his voice saying things I couldn't understand made a few appearances, along with Rudy's accusing gaze.

"I want an owl," the detective said suddenly. "That pep talk Archie gave you last night was pretty spot on. He's really started to be pretty useful." She took another sip of Joe's awesome coffee. "I want a bird who can keep an eye on things when I'm not there, too."

"You can take mine." When my phone vibrated, I looked down. Althea texted me and asked when I would stop by Arden's house. "Do we have a few minutes to see Althea before heading over to Cassandra?"

Emma nodded and then drained her coffee. "I'll just pay the check, and we can head out," she said, leaning out to get the attention of the waitress. "Hey! Can I have one of those to go?" Our waitress, Rose, held up five fingers and raised her eyebrow. "You got it. Five sugars."

"That's really disgusting," I told her. "You should just shoot up simple syrup if you're going to ingest that much sugar."

"I would, but that wouldn't taste nearly as

good." Emma texted someone and then looked up. "Captain's good. By the way, I was really impressed last night by how well you and Rex seemed to get along. When he first arrived, I assumed you two would fight at some point. At the fundraiser, you two were practically buddies."

Emma was correct. Rex and I used to be unable to stand each other. He'd snuck some of his blood into Emma so he could keep constant tabs on her like some psycho stalker, and I thought he was challenged in the "don't be evil" arena. We'd grown closer over time, and I trusted him.

Well, to a point.

He was still a vampire, after all.

We'd all spent the night in Rex's bunker the night before, with the vampires staying awake and the humans (and witches) sleeping in the front room. I trusted Rex to keep his front door locked and Damien relatively safe—or, at the very least, to alert me if anyone tried to break in. Everyone switched positions at sunrise.

Emma and I both wanted to speak with Ivy Masterson. Taylor Masterson, Ivy's mother, answered the phone as if she knew we would call. (Which, I mean, she was a psychic—so maybe she did.) She informed us she was happy to answer any questions we had about her daughter's situation and that if we didn't mind going into the darkened basement with her half-vampire child, Ivy would be happy to speak with us, too.

Jason offered to stay with Farah and Ami at the Sanguine Bunker to keep an eye on Rex and Damien. I gave Ami and Jason some Ministry magic beans—seeds, really—that could immobilize someone's feet in a massive twisted mess of thorny roots.

They're very effective—and, to be honest, not too bad as far as temporary prisons go. When deployed, alkaloids and hallucinogenic compounds are released in the dusty chaff. Some say that the colors in the fanciful visions it causes are quite lovely.

I gave no magic beans to Farah.

"Rex and I have managed to get along by meeting in the middle. I'll admit I didn't always like him—especially when he bonded you to him and lived in your head like a creeper. But," I said with a shrug. "I get why he did it. It was out of concern for you. He just went about it the wrong way."

Rose dropped off Emma's to-go coffee and grabbed the cash she left on the table. Once the waitress left, Emma smirked. "How generous of you."

"He knows that I'm not going to hurt his sister. And frankly, the way you run toward paranormal trouble, Emma, I think we're both grateful for the other."

"The way *I* run toward paranormal trouble?" She looked insulted. "Your mother picked this town to set up shop as Athena's current pope or whatever. My brother decided to build a vamp-friendly nightclub in Forkbridge, and as if that wasn't enough? He's adding a vampire hotel safe house thing to it. The pixies adopted the local heiress. A soldier I served with is a werewolf. Am I forgetting anything? Oh! Oh! The Orphic priest? Crazy Greek gods?"

I chuckled. "Okay, okay."

"You're damn right *okay*. You got a lot of nerve, Arden, acting like dealing with the paranormal is something *I* chased." Emma glared at me with affection. "You all came to me. The fact that I'm both alive and still human never ceases to amaze me."

I snorted.

Emma arched an eyebrow. "What?"

"Nothing," I said and shook my head. I had a thought about Emma's luck for the first time. "I was just thinking that maybe you *do* have a guardian angel who makes sure you don't get killed."

Emma looked up at the ceiling and mouthed something that looked like "thank you." Then she clasped her hands together and added, "And, you know, sorry. Really. I know I must be really challenging."

We both laughed.

* * *

"So, you don't need to tell us anything," Althea said as we walked into the house. "Aunt Gertie's been flying back and forth between here and Sanguine, keeping us updated on what's going on there." She put her hand on her hip. "Are you okay, by the way? Do you need an antidepressant potion? Or maybe a memory squasher potion? That whole thing with Rudy sounded like it was just awful."

"Is there anything you don't have a potion for?" Emma asked her. We walked down the hall toward the kitchen. The chandelier in the foyer had been turned on and was reflected by the mirror on the opposite wall, making the hall look twice as big.

"Me? I'm offended by the question. I have a potion for everything." Althea's eyes twinkled. "I'm that good."

Emma took another sip of her coffee. "Potion for everything, huh?"

One of the French doors opened, and my mother stepped out, a book in her hand. "Althea, the goddess doesn't like a braggart, and you most certainly do not have a potion for everything," she said, leveling a stern look at my sister. Aunt Gwennie followed her out and then closed the door behind her. "No one likes a show-off."

"Yes, ma'am," my sister mumbled.

My mother kept talking as we all headed toward the kitchen. "Gertie has been keeping us informed as to the drama at Sanguine," she repeated, with an even more concerned expression than Althea had managed. "Are you both all right?"

Emma and I both nodded. "We're fine, Mom."

"Everyone's doing just fine except for Killian Jarrow, who's dead, and Ivy Masterson, who's caught between being a human and being a vampire." Emma moved immediately toward the sugar bowl and dumped another spoonful in her already too sweet coffee. "Damien's fine for the moment, but that vampire slayer Farah is pretty much itching to cut him down." Emma stirred her coffee and then reached for the sugar spoon again. "If we solve this, we may condemn him. So…yeah, weird."

"Easy now," my mother told her. "That's a lot of sugar."

"I only have one spoonful in there," Emma told her innocently.

"Child, don't lie to a witch," my mother told Emma, her tone light and playful.

"Only a little one," Emma added, taking a sip and smiling.

My family lived in an old colonial-style home in the center of the small town of Forkbridge. Built in the late 1800s, it had had various families throughout the years before my grandmother made it a covenstead for our family.

One that, at eighteen, I couldn't wait to escape.

Despite this, there was something comforting about it now, especially after the emotions of last night and the dreams of the past that plagued me.

"Where's Archie?" Ayla (my youngest sister and the witch bonded to my deceased Aunt Gertie) said as she bounded into the kitchen. She was nearly a decade and a half my junior but was already taller and thinner than our mother. She had Mom's looks, but her personality was all her own.

"Good morning, Ayla," I said and hugged her.

"Good morning, little one." My mother leaned over and hugged her as well and then reached out to pull Emma away from the sugar bowl forcefully. "Emma, that's enough coffee and enough sugar. Have some chamomile tea instead."

Emma raised her coffee and shook it. "Are you kidding? This is only my third cup. I need at least five to function."

Ayla put her hands on her hips and looked at me with her head cocked to one side. "How are you even standing? Aunt Gertie's reports were making me tired, and all I had to do was listen to a report of the drama." She looked around, and before I could answer, she repeated, "Where's Archie? Aunt Gertie and I had an idea that she might be able to get him messages, and we wanted to try it."

"He's out hunting his breakfast," I told her. "And I'm standing because I slept last night." I turned to Althea. "Your vampire repellent potion was pretty useful. Jason and Ami were able to hang around without us worrying about them."

"What about the Farah woman?" Aunt Gwennie asked. "Is she helping at all?"

"If by helping you mean not making another attempt on Damien's life, then yes—she's helping," I said. "I didn't give her any of Althea's repellent. Since it works on all vampires, it would work on Rex, too, and we don't know at this point exactly how much we can trust her."

"I can make some that work on all vampires *other* than Rex if you want," Althea said. "It'll take me about five minutes."

My jaw dropped. "You can?"

She nodded. "Easy peasy. I still have Rex's blood from when we broke the blood bond he forced on Emma." She shot me a look and shook her head. "Honestly, for a witch, your lack of potion knowledge is appalling."

Okay, home and family being oddly comforting?

Slowly fading.

"You have his blood?" my mother asked Althea, her expression serious.

"Of course I do."

"You have his vampire blood," my mother repeated, her tone still deadly serious.

"I already said yes. What was I going to do with it, toss it in the trash so we get vampire rats? Throw it down the sink so we get vampire alligators? I mean, really, Mother." Althea put her hands on her hips. "That lack of knowledge about potions? You—"

"Althea, watch it," Aunt Gwennie said, her voice cracking like a whip.

"What? I was just—" Althea started to defend herself, but her voice trailed off when my mother's clear, green eyes met hers. "Okay, so, yeah," Althea said with less robust confidence and stepped back slightly, jerking her head in a nod. "Yeah, never mind. I'll get started on some repellent for Farah after I have a bite. I'm starving." She glanced at my mother. "Sorry."

"That's all right, dear," Mom said.

"Good girl," Aunt Gwennie murmured.

The atmosphere in the room changed, becoming more warm and welcoming. Althea smiled and relaxed as she looked at my mother, who beamed at her as if a switch had been flipped. Ayla, who had been watching the conversation with interest, resumed her breakfast as if nothing had happened.

"That's all right, dear. It was a late night for all of us," my mother told her. "Get some breakfast. You'll feel better." My mother nodded to the kitchen table, where a large plate held a mound of waffles, along with bacon and sausage links. Her eyes slid from Emma to me and back. "What else can we do to help you both?"

It was a shocking exchange in some ways.

My mother (the control freak who made sure my sisters were isolated and under her thumb every day I was gone) asked Emma and me what *we* needed from *her*.

No recriminations, no lectures about safety. No criticisms of Ayla for getting information about our case, no attacks on me for leaving Ami in a vampire lair.

Don't get me wrong. My mother's love was unconditional—but her caring and compassion were as vast as her will to take over every aspect of our lives and shield us from everything that could give us so much as a finger splinter.

She'd grown in the year since I'd come home.

So had I.

As I told her about our plans to visit Cassandra and promised to keep in touch, I wondered if the goddess Athena's "gift" hadn't been for her as well.

* * *

"Ivy?"

The shadows of the wine cellar were quiet and

peaceful. Jars of wine lined the walls like gold bricks encased in a mini-fortress. Ivy sat in the back room, her eyes like dark, hard candy. She looked composed but tense.

"Hello," she said, a hissing, machine gun rhythm like an angry rattlesnake slithering through the bramble.

I nodded once. "Hi, Ivy."

The half-vampire's lips were dry and cracked. She was dressed in gray sweatpants and a gray shirt that needed to be washed, and her feet were busy digging something out from beneath a pile of old blankets. The room smelled like old books, dust, and a faint floral scent.

"Oh, dear God," Emma whispered, her voice unable to hide her shock. "You've been like this since Halloween? That's some eight months now."

Emma was right. It was June.

Eight months.

Ivy, as composed and calm as she appeared, was a picture of desperate heartbreak.

"Yes. But I will not drink blood," she whispered raspingly. "I didn't ask for this. I don't want to be this. His blood may have turned me, but I don't have to let it change me. I don't care what it takes. I'll stay down here for years if I have to. I'm not going to feed on anyone, and I will *not* kill any innocents. I can fight it." Ivy's eyes narrowed. "I don't care what it does to me. I will not drink blood."

Taylor's eyes showed the months of accumulated exhaustion as Ivy's mother spread her hands in a gesture of helplessness. "My beautiful, stubborn girl," she whispered. "This should never have happened to you."

A small tabby cat streaked by my knees as it raced into Ivy's open arms, where it settled. She nuzzled its fur, and the cat purred like a miniature motor engine. Its large, judgmental eyes were like saucers as it looked at me accusingly.

"I have to try," I told Emma. She didn't even ask what I meant.

"Can you?" she asked quietly. "Can you change her back?

"I don't know," I said. "I'm going to try."

Ivy placed the cat gently on the floor, stood up, and walked over to a jar of wine on the wall. She twisted the lid, popped it, and took a long drink of the bottle without taking a breath. "My mother's told me about you," she whispered after swallowing and then chugged from the bottle again. "I can't believe lightning magic is pleasant to be on the other end of." She wiped her mouth with her sleeve, looked across the room at her mother, and then said "I'll do whatever you want. Just get rid of this."

I looked down to see the cat (now curled up on Ivy's chair) staring at me. I'm not sure why the goddess bestowed the gift of speech on Archie. With a glance, animals could convey their opinion quite clearly.

"Please, Ms. Arden," Ivy begged.

I looked up at the half-vampire. "I have to be honest with you. I don't know what will happen if I try to change you back. This magic...it doesn't always work the way I expect it to."

The cat yawned.

"If I die, I die," Ivy said with a resigned shrug. "As determined as I am, I know at some point I might not be able to control myself, and I'll kill someone. Maybe someone I love. I know that." Ivy looked at her mother, and a chill seemed to run through the room. "It hurts to have this blood inside me. It feels like...like I'm being eaten alive from the inside out." She looked at me with eyes full of anguish. "Please. I can't live like this. I'd rather be dead than live like this."

Taylor looked at her daughter and then turned to me. "I'll do whatever you need to help you if she crosses the veil. Just get rid of this. End her suffering one way or another. Please."

Emma and I looked at each other.

I nodded.

The lightning bolt arced from my hands and reached out toward Ivy Masterson before I actually fully committed to the decision. It crackled and arched across the entire length of the room as if looking for her. She screamed and reached out toward the sizzling energy, but the magic danced just out of her reach. "No! Please!" she sobbed as she watched it pull away. "Help me!"

Determination, desperation, and a hint of grief were all reflected in her face as she flung herself toward the bright, blazing light. As her hand wrapped around the bolt, Ivy gasped. As if their touch had set it into motion, the lightning spread out and wrapped around her, cocooning her in its warmth. The fear in her eyes turned to wonder.

Then she closed her eyes.

Oh, you have to be kidding, I thought, my stomach jumping in a panic.

I gasped and watched as the tension in her face faded and disappeared before my eyes. An incantation came to my mind unspoken, and a rush of power ran through me as I willed the magic to flow from my hands, through her body, cleansing her, making her whole. Focusing on the massive power that trembled in my fingertips. I pictured her as healthy and strong. She would move and speak, free of pain and weakness.

Suddenly, with a jolt, Ivy tensed one more time and opened her eyes.

Emma stood frozen in place, unable to move.

Ivy smiled. Her face lit up, the color returning as the crackling magic faded away. With a last flash of light, she screamed once, twitches and spasms rattling her body. Then, darkness. With a soft laugh, Ivy collapsed to the ground.

The world stopped.

The magic stopped.

I felt it all drain out of me.

"No!" I shouted, terrified I'd just killed the poor girl. "Ivy? Ivy!"

Emma grabbed me, pointing. "It's okay, Astra. She's fine," she said firmly. "She's fine. Look. Look at her! She's fine."

"Sorry. Sorry about the scream." The cat, now standing on its back legs, front paws on Ivy's shoulder, leaped into the half-vampire's arms. She hugged it tightly and kissed its head. "I'm fine. More than fine, in fact. I am still a half-vampire," she said, her voice weak as she lifted her head. "But your light has taken the hunger and the pain from me." The tension on her face was gone, and she had a gentleness to her eyes that hadn't been there before. "It's gone."

"I'm so sorry if I hurt you," I told Ivy.

The cat looked at me and, with a loud yawn, crawled out of Ivy's arms and walked away, bored.

Taylor raced over to embrace her daughter. "Oh, Ivy," she said, her voice muffled as she held her daughter. "Oh, Ivy."

Ivy looked at me, her head on her mother's shoulder, with eyes that shone with gratitude. "I owe you—"

"Nothing," I said emphatically, embarrassed that the goddess's magic had taken away the symptom but not the disease. I was angry that I wasn't able to give this girl back her life after eight months in a wine cellar. Eight months of suffering, hunger, of misery.

Yes, sure, I was glad I was able to take the pain of what was happening to her away.

But it was still happening to her.

CHAPTER EIGHT

"*S*ometimes I wonder if it's actually a curse to be as strong as I am," Ivy said with an embarrassed little half-smile as she sat down next to a marble tasting table. "My friends have always told me that I hold up so well under strain they wonder if I'm a robot. I'm not a robot," she adds with another smile. "I've just always held up under stress." Her grin turned into a faint grimace. "I wasn't sure I could do it this time, though."

We sat around the tasting table, the recessed pot lighting of the wine cellar dimmed to give the chat an oddly intimate ambiance. The soft purr of the cooling system was the only sound in the lower level of the psychic's house.

"You've always had determination, Ivy," Taylor said proudly. She looked at her daughter with a loving gaze, the pride of a mother oozing through every pore of her skin. "And you've always done the right thing."

"Not always, but with the big stuff, I try. Well, you'd know if I hadn't," she responded. "The ghosts would have told you." Ivy scrunched her face up in irritation. "I didn't do the right thing on Halloween, though. That's how I got into this mess in the first place."

"Can you tell us what happened with Killian and Damien on Halloween?" Emma asked, seizing the statement to push questioning as she reached in her bag and pulled out her notebook. "I've been told that they turned you against your will, but not much more than that."

"It never would have happened if the ghosts had been around," Taylor jumped in before Ivy could speak, her voice dripping with a vengeance. I wasn't sure if she was angry at the ghosts, the vampires, or both. "They would have known what was happening, and they would have stopped it. I know the guru said vampires had nothing to do with their disappearance, but I almost wonder if—"

"Mother, the guru wouldn't lie to you," Ivy

interrupted, defending the spiritualists' leader. "I know you're trying to find some rhyme or reason for what happened, but it wasn't complicated. I drank too much, and I chose to bring home people I couldn't trust. That's all."

Taylor's lips twisted as she leaned forward in her chair, her expression dark. "Maybe there was more going on than the fires. Maybe turning you was the way they attacked me. Maybe he—"

"No, Mother." Ivy looked down at the marble and ran her finger along the veins of the table, her face resigned to the truth as she saw it. "You didn't see the condition I was in. I know what happened was my fault, and I have to take responsibility for my actions. It had nothing to do with that whole drama with the arson and the jeweler and…no, Mama. I just made a terrible mistake."

I watched Ivy struggle with an inner battle, trying to overcome the guilt she felt for the suffering she (and her mother) had endured. "What happened to you wasn't your fault. Even if you made one bad, irresponsible choice after another worse, even more irresponsible choice, it *still* wouldn't be your fault," I told her, my tone gentle. "It was up to Damien and Killian to get your consent. If they didn't, that's on them. Not you."

"Even if you have to deal with the consequences, Astra's right," Emma added. "It wasn't your fault."

Ivy's expression softened. "Thanks...I guess." She gave a semi-shrug, her eyes turning sad. "I just hate it. I hate the idea that they took control over me like that. I hate feeling weak."

"You're not weak," Taylor insisted. "You're strong and smart and beautiful. Yes, you made some mistakes." She looked at her daughter with a critical eye. "You have to take responsibility for your actions, yes. You should not have drunk so much. You should not have brought them back here. But these two women are right. What ultimately happened was not your fault. It was theirs." Her eyes flared, and her jaw set, her face hard as stone. "And don't you forget it."

"You certainly didn't," I said. "Is it true you hired Farah Hutter, a vampire hunter, to kill Damien Elkhart?"

Taylor's eyes turned cold and hard. "I wanted Damien dead, yes."

"Mother!" Ivy looked shocked at her mom's murderous intentions. "You didn't!"

"I just said I wanted him dead. I didn't say I

did anything about it," she told her daughter noncommittally.

"I can't arrest you for trying to kill a vampire," Emma told her. "They don't officially exist."

Funny how assuring someone there are no consequences brings out their true beliefs about their own behavior. Before Emma finished her statement, Taylor Masterson's face lit up like the Fourth of July.

"I most certainly *did* hire a retributionist to wipe that man from the face of the earth!" she said. Her face was a warped mask of excitement and murderous intentions. "Damien had hurt you, Ivy, and I wasn't about to sit around and do nothing. It had been eight months." She looked at her daughter with pleading eyes. "It wasn't just retribution. I hoped by killing him you would come back to your humanity. You know, like in that Gary Oldman movie. Kill the sire, the vampire children that haven't fully turned go back to being normal."

"Well, at least she's telling the truth," I said to Emma.

"Me?" Taylor asked.

"No," I told her. "Farah. We met her last night at the fundraiser at Sanguine. Well, *met* may be too casual a word. She tried to kill Damien in the middle of the club, and I stopped her." I briefly explained to the psychic about the star card and that Damien was the current object of my divine mission. "She's agreed to wait until the star card goes out to kill him."

"I'm not convinced she's being totally honest, though. She still could have killed Killian before coming into the club. Just because some of what she said is turning out to be true doesn't mean she can be totally trusted," Emma pointed out. Turning to Taylor, she asked, "Why send Farah after just Damien? Why not Killian and Damien?"

"Why not kill all three, you mean?" Taylor asked.

"Hold up—three?" I blinked. "What do you mean three? There was a third vampire here that night?"

Ivy nodded.

Great.

"Maybe you should start at the beginning," Taylor urged her daughter.

With a deep sigh of resignation, Ivy told us the whole long, sordid story. Well, a short story, really—with eight months of consequences.

* * *

HER MEMORY of Halloween was a blur, but Ivy did the best she could to recall what happened. "I was out of control. I know that—it's hard to remember details. I had too much to drink. I mean, it was my first Halloween being over twenty-one, right?" She blushed, her pale face flushing too deeply pink to be fully human. "I went to Ronna Phillips's party, and she had a lot of alcohol. I think all the psychics were just too distracted, and we…well, to be honest, we took advantage of the ghosts being gone and our parents being somewhere else."

"The youngsters of Cassandra went a little wild," Taylor admitted, her face drawn. "They knew the ghosts weren't watching, and the adults were obsessed with finding the ghosts."

"We weren't youngsters, Mom. We were all adults."

"Then perhaps you all should have acted like it."

Cassandra was an odd little Central Florida town with the world's highest number of psychics per capita. Over the years, ghosts had gathered here because of how many people they could talk to, and it had become famous all over the world for its incredible medium (and spectral) density—and its massive Halloween festival.

But last Halloween, the ghosts disappeared.

Crowds still came to Cassandra's Halloween festival, but mediums all over town called across the veil and received no response. Those ghosts had served as the town's sentries; without them on patrol, a series of arson fires had destroyed the homes of the most prominent mediums.

That's not even mentioning the hippie-dippie new agers' belief that anything that caught fire wanted to catch fire.

Anyway, the point is?

The town is weirder than Forkbridge, if you can believe it.

"At the party, Damien approached me in the kitchen," Ivy said. "He was sad, complaining about Killian and Adriana, two friends that he'd come with, and how they had no idea how much seeing them together here hurt him. I listened to him." She shifted on her chair. "I think he said he used to live with them or live with her or something, and then when they met, he was 'tossed aside' like he didn't mean anything."

"Did you say Adriana?" I asked, a little shocked. "Adriana Kingsley was there that night?" Ivy nodded. I looked at Emma. "Adriana is the sire of both Damien and Killian."

"I know. I was there last night when Farah explained it all, remember?"

"Oh, right." I frowned.

Emma turned back to Ivy. "Okay, let's fast forward from the party. When you came back here to your house, who was with you?"

"Killian, Damien, and Adriana. Honestly, I felt pretty safe with Adriana even though I didn't know them. She was really nice and, well, you never think another woman is going to put you in danger or anything."

"Did you know they were vampires?" I asked.

Another shake of her head. "Not until they got into the fight."

Emma and I both perked up like meerkats standing on top of a dirt mound. "Fight?" we asked in unison.

Ivy nodded. "We came down here so I could show them the wine cellar. I'd told Adriana about it back at the party, and she'd been all interested in it." The young woman frowned. "I think she was more interested in it because there was no sun down here, honestly. She didn't seem to know much about wine. But I didn't know what they were at the time. When they got here, they asked if they could stay and sleep it off, and I said yes. Though it was a little weird. They didn't seem drunk."

Emma nodded once. "Where was your mother while this was going on?"

"She was with the other psychics," Ivy said, her eyes slanting toward Taylor. "A few groups decided to meet in different places to try and contact the ghosts across the veil. They were getting worried. So she wasn't home."

The psychic nodded, her lips pressed into a thin line. "I should have been."

"You're lucky you weren't," I told her. "You might have been turned as well."

Taylor's face paled.

"When we first got here, Adriana went down to explore the wine cellar, and they followed. I stayed up here because I was tired, and I'd had too much to drink. The next thing I know, I hear a scream. I rushed down there and found the vampires on top of each other, snarling and snapping and pushing at each other."

Emma nodded and wrote something in her notebook. "Okay. So you came downstairs and saw the three vampires in your wine cellar fighting. Then what happened? Could you tell what they were fighting about?"

"It's all so hazy," Ivy said, her eyes cast down at

her lap. "And I was so frightened. I was drunk, and I saw their fangs, and...I mean, I grew up in Cassandra, and so things that are unseen by most people are kind of normal for me. But vampires?" Ivy's eyes darted to her mother. "I didn't know they were real. Sorry."

Emma reached across the table and patted the young woman's hand. "Don't be sorry. It's not your fault." Emma looked at me with raised brows. "Can you?"

"Can she what?" Taylor asked, looking alarmed.

"Astra's a psycho...psycho..." Emma frowned, trying to remember the word.

"My inherited power is *psychometry*," I said, casting a vicious glare at Emma.

"Right, that." Emma pointed. "She can grab your hand and try and relate what you saw that night, or you can show us the room this happened in, and she can try to read the room."

"Your hand would be better since you're thinking about it," I told her, nodding. "You've been down here for eight months and pacing these rooms in misery. That's a lot of layers of energy and trauma to shove on the walls."

Ivy extended her hand toward me without hesitation. I took it.

Then I closed my eyes and gave it my best shot.

Emma asked Ivy a question, and I tried to tune her out. The room suddenly smelled of vanilla and cinnamon. I could feel a strange heaviness in the air, like the weight of the vampire's fury had a density to it. I took a few more deep breaths and tried to focus through the thick haze of angry emotions.

"Damien is pleading with Adriana to take him back," I told them, my words dragging slowly out of my mouth as my mind tried to interpret the jumble of images and sounds in my head. "But Killian is threatening him. Damien calls Killian jealous, and Killian calls Damien a name I'm not going to repeat."

Emma frowned. "Damien is calling *Killian* jealous?"

Ivy shook slightly as if shrugging. "I don't know."

I ran my hand over my forehead and tried to concentrate. "He loves her. He's begging her to take him back. He'll do anything. Adriana is shouting at him," I continued, still feeling like I was watching an odd dream. "She says he's weak and stupid, and she doesn't want him now. She says he's a sniveling little boy and that if he messed up the last time, then he'd better damn well make the next time worth her while."

"Wait, who's the *he* in this scenario?" Emma asked. "Killian or Damien?"

I frowned. "Killian."

"Adriana would take Killian *back*? I thought they were together, and Damien was the one pining to get back into the poly vamp triad?"

I didn't answer. "Killian's saying he needs to leave the city and the state. Atlanta. He's afraid someone's going to find out that he's a vampire." I paused, trying to make sense of the jumbled mess in my mind. "But Adriana's telling him she's not going to leave with him. She's saying she can't." I paused. "She's not saying why."

"What the heck happened in Atlanta?" Emma murmured. She sounded far away.

"Adriana tells them both to prove themselves to her," I said, wincing as I saw her point to Ivy. "She told them to give her Ivy for her nest. That she likes the look of the girl. Ivy screams no," I said, wincing again. I felt her fingers twitch. It was the only outward sign of her distress. "Killian looks horrified. He refuses. Damien—" I released Ivy's hand like it was on fire and opened my eyes. It lingered in the air for a second before she let it drop to the table. "As we know," I said, "Damien doesn't."

The room was deafeningly quiet, the air thick once again—this time, with the weight of what had happened.

* * *

"I DON'T GET IT. If Adriana wanted Ivy, why did she leave her here?" Emma asked. "And what on earth were they talking about? It didn't sound like a lover's quarrel. It sounded like a conspiracy that had gone wrong somehow." Emma tapped her pen on her notebook, her expression pensive as she tried to make some sense of the night's events and the memories Ivy had shared through me.

Ivy shook her head, her eyes wide. "I don't know. I wish I understood more, but Astra was able to make more sense of my own mind than I've been able to all these months."

"Was it a test of loyalty of some kind?" I wondered.

"What loyalty?" Emma countered. "He's here. Killian was here. She's in Atlanta. Damien was here, too, so he didn't get anything out of it."

Emma's words were a jolt. "Yeah, so we think,"

I said slowly. "But is she in Atlanta? Did he get nothing?"

"Good point," Emma said, her frown deepening. "We need to know what happened in Atlanta. And with everything going on here, we can't just take a road trip up to Georgia." She looked at me. "You know what that means, right?"

I didn't even have to say it out loud. We had access to only one person that might have had a clear head during the fight and probably knows this conspiracy. Damien Elkhart. I didn't even like being in the same room with the sleaze bag. Grabbing his hand and reading his innermost thoughts?

Ugh. "Yeah. I know."

"If they'd left Killian's body, you could have read him."

"Killian is really dead?" Ivy asked.

"So far as I can tell," Emma replied. Emma turned toward Taylor. "I have to ask you, though. Why Damien only? Why not send someone after Killian or Adriana?"

"Damien was the one that bit Ivy, and with her blood tie to him, she could give me information about him but not about the others," Taylor explained. "The ghosts found out who all three of them were using that information, but…I'm really not a vengeful woman, Detective Sullivan," the woman said with a small, uncomfortable smile. "Yes, as a mother, a part of me wanted Damien dead because of what he'd done. But my goal was to free my daughter. I gave her life once. I am determined to do it once more."

"Will that work?" Emma asked me.

"I don't know. I…I honestly don't think so." I didn't want to tell them what I did know because it wasn't good. "While vampires are connected by the blood like a big web, one strand getting cut doesn't collapse it or even a part of it. I can't think of any legitimate reason feeding or not feeding would change the vampiric infection inside Ivy, and likewise, I can't think of why killing the sire would make the vampire venom in her disappear," I explained. I looked at Ivy. "You're not *really* a half-vampire. You're just taking a super long time to make your full transition, that's all."

Ivy nodded. Her skin was pale, and her eyes downcast. Her mother put her arm around her and squeezed, looking stricken.

Emma was quiet, her expression solemn. "Can we help her change back?"

"Althea might be able to come up with something," I said, my expression forcing a hopefulness I didn't exactly feel. If my magic divine electric boogaloo couldn't wipe it out, what hope was there for a potion? But instead, I said, "She was able to get Rex's blood out of you, so she's probably studied this more than any of us."

"Will you ask her?" Taylor whispered.

I nodded.

"Thank you," Ivy said gratefully.

I nodded again, feeling like a heel.

CHAPTER NINE

The tires of the car squealed against the concrete as Emma hit the gas. Archie followed above and to the side of us, his head cocked to the side like he was trying to figure out what was going on. Emma and I didn't speak as she steered the car along the wooded road. We were each lost in our own thoughts.

"Can I ask you something?" Emma asked about halfway home. "And I don't want you to take this the wrong way."

"Sure."

The sharp turn of her head toward me and the harsh glint in her eyes put me on alert unexpectedly. "Are paranormals just more likely to be inherently criminal?" Emma exhaled, her expression unreadable, and then forced her eyes back on the road. "You told me that there was a parallel world living alongside mine, and I thought you were being metaphorical." She took her eyes off the road long enough to look at me directly again. "What Damien did, what Adriana encouraged him to do...I just don't understand. Are their natures inherently...I don't know, insensitive?"

"That wasn't insensitivity, what Damien did. That was sociopathic."

"Fine. Let me rephrase my question and drop the politeness. Are most paranormals psychos?" she asked, her tone exasperated. "You and I see the world differently from each other, but I doubt that you would ever do something that cruel without knowing what you were doing. Right?" She glanced back at me for a moment, gauging my expression, and then looked back at the road.

"Did you know that luxury car drivers are more likely to cut off other drivers and ignore pedestrians entering crosswalks?" I asked Emma (instead of directly answering her question.)

She shook her head.

"They are. Wealthier people physically react

less when shown a video of children with cancer. Studies say they're consistently worse at reading the emotions of others. Did you know just thinking about your own money, concentrating on your own abundance and everything you have, makes you humans less willing to share candy with children?" I paused. "Candy. With *children*."

Her eyes widened. "You're making this up."

"I'm not. The study was published. Peer-reviewed. There's a great article about it in *Scientific American*," I said with a resigned tone. "As humans grow wealthier or more powerful, their compassion toward others goes down. The researchers tried to figure out if selfishness leads to wealth and power, or the wealth and power produces selfishness." I tapped my finger on the dashboard. "They think it's the latter—that wealth and abundance give us a sense of freedom and independence from others. The less we rely on others, the less we may be concerned about their feelings." I turned. "Paranormals aren't that different from humans."

The detective frowned as she thought about my words. "Well, that's depressing. It does explain Palm Beach, though."

"It really is crazy. The more you can do for people, the less you want to do it. I mean, let's face it—most people don't realize how good they have it. Did you know if you take home more than $34,000 a year, give or take, you are among the top 1 percent globally?"

"That can't be right."

"Nonetheless, it is. Around the world, approximately three billion people live on less than $2 per day. Someone earning that in this country is likely to feel as if they are struggling, but on this planet? They are not, in fact, the 99 percent."

"That, also, is pretty depressing."

"The 1 percent is much different than most people realize." I waved my hand, realizing I was getting sidetracked. "That has nothing to do with your question, really. I just thought that was fascinating."

"Okay, and the answer to my question?"

"We have the same problem. We're elite. We're the most powerful beings on the planet," I told her. "No one can become us—well, most of us. We live longer, we accumulate more money, we have more insight, we have a deeper understanding of the world and how it really works, we have better defenses, and we have better offenses. Hell, we can even travel cheaper. We are, in our minds, superior in every way to humans—and we're sure of that because a good portion of us can read your minds." I explained without a touch of embarrassment. "Knowing that, why would we think we needed to follow your rules?"

"Because you're just better," Emma said dryly.

"We're so much better; it's like we're a different species," I admitted. "At least that's how a lot of us look at it. Not me, at least not precisely like that." I sighed. "Look, there's no way you'll ever understand how paranormals think."

"Because?"

"Because it comes with a level of arrogance, selfishness, cruelty, or self-regard, unlike anything you've ever seen in a human."

Emma was quiet for a while, taking in what I said. "You know, Arden, what you say may be true. But I have to point one thing out," she said as she pulled into the driveway at Arden House. She put the car in park, turned off the engine, and turned to stare at me with a sad expression on her face. "If your superiority comes with arrogance, selfishness, cruelty, or a self-regard so all-encompassing you can't see or care about the damage you do to others? In my book, you're not really superior to us." She paused. "Not at all."

Emma had chosen her words with care and appeared to use the word *you* deliberately. She waited for me to respond to the polite slam, to defend paranormals despite the destruction she'd seen with her own eyes wrought by those with no care and no conscience.

But I didn't.

There was no point.

Realizing I would not respond, Emma grabbed her keys and headed out of the car, closing the door behind her with a slam.

"IT's HER BROTHER," Archie said as he circled down and landed on my shoulder. The owl swiveled his head to maintain balance as he sensed the subtle movements of the wind and then walked down my arm. "The last time she got involved with vampires, they were the victims, right? Now they're the perpetrators." He clicked his beak as she walked into Arden House without me and shut the front door behind her. "If

Damien's this bad, I think she's wondering what her brother Rex is now."

"And you know this how?" I asked, surprised.

Archie's body relaxed as he perched in my hand, and his head bobbed up and down as he said, "I am incredibly insightful."

"You sensed all this staring at the roof of her car?"

"Owls have hearing the best of *any* animal tested. Ever. In the history of the world, even."

Sure they did. "You could hear us talking?"

"What, you didn't read that in *Scientific American* while you were scanning articles on human class warfare?" Archie suddenly shifted his weight, turning his head to peer around me with his unblinking eyes. "Actually, you and I have developed a new power. Or, well, *I* have." He clicked his beak. "I doubt it has anything to do with you. I could hear everything that went on in that basement like I was sitting on your shoulder. Same thing in the car."

A customer carrying a large bag exited the converted garage that housed Athena's Garden, the new age shop my family owned. His gaze was drawn to my feathered companion and me as he passed through the front yard. Once he processed what he was seeing and hearing, the man came to a halt and just stared, open-mouthed.

I stared back. Then I waved. "Hi!"

Archie hooted aggressively. "Go away, mortal!" The owl swiveled his head to peer at me with his golden eyes. "I don't know why your mother keeps that store open. Half the time, it's closed for a star card emergency, anyway." Archie glared at the man. "Like it should have been today."

The man, who'd heard a series of clicks and hoots instead of Archie's insults—but clearly read the aggression in Archie's tone—gave both of us an uncertain nod, raised his hand in a half-wave, and quickly continued down the walkway before he could think too much about it.

"You really need to stop acting like a predatory owl with the customers, dude," I said as I watched the man struggle to get the keys to his Lexus door. "Mom loves the store, and the townies already think we're crazy over here."

Archie puffed up his chest. His voice was shrill as he waggled his tail feathers. "You make me sound like some barnyard animal instead of a majestic owl of the goddess." He cocked his head back and forth like he was having an internal debate with himself. "I'm the goddess's own owl.

Not even you have as much freedom as me. I say whatever I want whenever I want."

"Whatever you say, Archimedes," I said, amused, as the man pulled away from the curb with a screech of expensive tires. "Okay, back to the discussion. You could hear everything from the air." I asked, turning my head to look at the owl. "Since you heard it all, do you have any thoughts on what's going on with the vampires?"

"It's a conspiracy," he said darkly.

"Of?"

Archie shifted his weight from side to side, and his wings opened and closed as he adjusted. "How would I know? That's your area. Just because I'm the owl of the goddess doesn't mean I know everything." He paused, then added with a defensive nod, "Besides, you know what they say."

"What do they say?"

Archie blinked. "Well, I guess you *don't* know what they say."

I stared and raised an eyebrow.

"Fine," he said, and he clicked his beak. "They say the gods help those who help themselves."

"You mean 'God helps those who help themselves.' I think Benjamin Franklin said that—"

"No. No! You're not doing that this time,"

Archie said with an angry little hoot, his talons clutching me tightly. "That came from ancient Greece. Sophocles said, 'No good e'er comes of leisure purposeless; And heaven ne'er helps the men who will not act.'And Euripides said, 'Try first thyself, and after call in God; For to the worker God himself lends aid.' Aesop even wrote a fable about Athena! Did you know that?" Archie's beak opened wide as he shot its point home, and then it closed shut with an audible click. "Did you? Guy's ship is wrecked, and he calls on Athena to help him. Do you know what she told him? Huh? Do you?"

I stared at the riled-up Archie silently and waited for his tantrum to pass.

"She told that idiot to try swimming first!" he hooted triumphantly. Archie flapped his wings to emphasize his point as if he was trying to flee but was stopped by some unseen tether. "So, no. Benjamin Franklin did not come up with that at all. No way. No, ma'am. Nope. Didn't happen."

A car slowed in front of Arden House, and a family stared at the goddess's very own owl's dressing down of me through their darkened car windows. I forced a smile and waved cheerfully. They accelerated and drove on down the road.

"Archie, we need to go inside. We're attracting attention."

"I always attract attention. I'm stunning," Archie muttered. "You, on the other hand, look like some run of the mill mortal trying to bend the Florida wilderness to your will." Archie turned his head and looked at me. "Not even a particularly well-dressed mortal. When everyone told you to stop wearing your uniform, no one advised you to switch to—"

"You know, jellyfish have lived for 600 million years, and they don't even have a brain," I said to Archie in a calm, friendly tone. "That must give you hope."

Archie froze.

Then he blinked.

Then he blinked again.

The owl tilted his head, and his expression softened. "I don't know whether to be proud or insulted."

"You'll figure it out," I said, and I went up to the door.

* * *

"Here's the potion for the slayer," Althea said, handing me a glass bottle containing a clear, bubbly liquid with a light pink hue. "Now, that's a twofer," she explained, her expression serious. "It's going to give her defense against vampires other than Rex, and it's going to force her to tell you the truth until the next full moon." I raised my eyebrow. "Aunt Gertie told Ayla, who told me, obviously."

Aunt Gertie (the nosy family ghost) was becoming quite useful.

"Which is when?" I asked.

Althea looked confused. "What?"

"The full moon. When is it? When does this stop working?"

"Oy, how did I get stuck with you?" Archie snarked. "You're a witch, and you don't even know when the next full moon takes place?"

"Do you know when the next full moon is?" I asked him.

"Of course I do. It's when the moon has moved in its orbit so that Earth is between the moon and the sun. Like, again," he said with a toss of his feathered head. "You know, the next time it does that. It happens every month."

I stared at the owl, daring Archie to continue.

"The between thing," he said slowly. "That's when it is."

"Are you done?"

He swallowed.

"We just had the full moon two days ago, Astra," Althea said, her voice lowering so my mother wouldn't hear that her oldest witch daughter (and the divine owl riding on her shoulder) had no idea when the next full moon would happen. "The Buck Moon is July 13th. And it's in Capricorn, so the potion's potency will probably fade over the course of the whole day instead of happening all at once."

I nodded and slipped the potion into my pocket. "Did Emma or Ayla say anything about what happened to Ivy?" I asked my sister.

Thea shook her head.

"The girl that was turned against her will? She's spent eight months not drinking any blood in hopes that she could get rid of the vampiric infection before it fully turned her."

"Well, that's a good thing, right?" Althea asked.

"Good, except she's not living any life. She can't be human. She doesn't want to be a vampire. She's stuck in some horrible limbo living in her mother's wine cellar." I leaned against the wall. "I mean, it was a beautiful wine cellar, but I wouldn't want to spend eternity down there."

"You claimed you had a potion for everything," Archie said to Thea, his eyes twinkling. "Time to put your herbs and magic where your mouth is, my immodest teen potion master. Let's get to it. Show us you really can strut sitting down."

"You've gone back to being saucy, Archie," my sister said, tossing her ponytail back over her shoulder and putting a hand on her hip. "Well, not that you ever really stopped. But you're back to—"

Archie glared fiercely at her, shutting her up with one look. He glanced at me. "Is she all hat and no cattle?" Before I could answer, the owl turned back to Thea and snapped, "Can you do it or not?"

"She can do it," Ayla, my youngest sister, said as she walked up to us. "Althea's invented potions other witches never even had the brains to think of." Ayla's eyes were unfocused, as if she was listening to a voice only she could hear. Then she nodded. "Aunt Gertie says we—Althea and me—need to go see Ivy Masterson, and she can show us which book you'll need for reference."

"How does she know about turning or turning back vampires?" I asked.

"Now, don't flip out, okay?" Ayla met my eyes. "Killian found her."

The shock at a vampire ghost hanging out

with my dead witch aunt beyond the veil was almost enough to make my knees give out on me. Vampires don't turn into ghosts—or so we'd been taught at the Ministry.

"Killian?" I echoed dumbly. "But I thought vampires lost their souls when they turned? Isn't that their whole story, the whole vampire schtick? That they're soulless?"

"Killian says apparently not because his soul is in the afterlife hanging with Aunt Gertie," Ayla told me. "And before you ask me, Mom confirmed it. He's here. It really is him."

"Emma and I should interview him through you."

Althea glanced out the window. "Does it have to be right now? It's going to be sundown in about two hours. Aunt Gertie told us some vampire from Atlanta already showed up here to investigate. If that's the case, I should probably get to Cassandra before nightfall. I'm going to need to ward that basement just in case." She raised her eyebrow. "Otherwise, I'll have to wait until tomorrow."

"Yeah, that's a good idea. He's from the Ambrogio, by the way," I said, nodding. "I don't know if that helps with your warding or not."

"Astra knew him in the military," Archie

added. He pressed his beak together and shook his head. "Their reunion wasn't exactly warm and fuzzy."

"Wait. What? You had vampires in the military?" Ayla asked, her eyes wide.

"Rudy wasn't a vampire then." I turned to Ayla. "Has Killian said anything about who killed him? He must have seen who stabbed him."

Ayla shook her head no. "Your Ministry knife is kind of genius in a terrifying, horrible way. Not only does it block the other vampires from knowing someone died, but it also blocks the murdered person from knowing who stabbed them. All Killian saw was a knife coming toward him. Like, a disembodied knife floating in the air, and then whammo. Death." She paused, frowning. "Well, death again."

"Invisibility," I muttered. "That makes sense." The Ministry had a lot of tools that obfuscated their hand in things. A murder weapon that cloaks the murderer didn't strike me as surprising.

"People you went after didn't have a chance, did they?" Althea said it as a statement more than a question. Her expression was one of revolted sadness, eyes clouded, brows down in a shocked scowl.

"Hey, Thea," Ayla said with a toss of her head. "Astra didn't forge the thing."

"There's a reason there was a rebellion to take down the Witches' Council." I pushed away from the wall and quickly changed the subject. "Is there any news on what was going on in Atlanta? Surely Killian must have known about that."

"I wrote some notes down for you," Ayla said, nodding. "In the kitchen. What's the deal with the Ambrogio, by the way? From what Killian said, they sound like the Volturi or something."

"What's a Volturi?" I asked.

Ayla looked at me, her eyes wide. "Astra, come on. It's the vampire royal family from the Twilight series."

"The Twilight books," I said and frowned. "I've vaguely heard of them."

"Wait a minute." Althea stopped walking and turned to Ayla. "Maybe the Ambrogio aren't like the Volturi. Maybe the *Volturi* are like the *Ambrogio*." The two stared at one another, their eyes sparkling with excitement. "Hey. Question. Have you ever seen Rex sparkle?" she asked, motioning her hand toward me. "Or any vampire sparkle?"

Suddenly, Ayla winced.

Althea looked concerned. "What's the matter? What happened?"

"Killian would like us to drop the subject."

"Because we're right?" the potion master asked excitedly.

"No." Ayla winced again. "No. Definitely not. He says quite emphatically that we are not right about anything we're saying."

CHAPTER TEN

I assumed that the next item on the agenda would be an interview with Killian Jarrow via my sister, Ayla. Unfortunately, vampires appear to be as annoying in death as they are in life—the vampire ghost refused to focus on anything but Ivy Masterson's desire to return to the human side of life.

"If he's not going to talk, he's not going to talk. Call us if you need us, then. I guess," Emma told Ayla, her expression confused by Killian's refusal. She shook her head slowly, then looked at me briefly with a raised eyebrow. "We're going to head back over to Rex's bunker, but we can be here faster than you think." She fixed her gaze on my sisters. "And don't invite in any vampires."

"Oh, that won't be a problem," Ms. Masterson assured us, her eyes darting sideways, taking in the darkening shadows of the quiet street in front of the Masterson house. "The guru called your mother for assistance the day after Ivy was turned." She made a motion toward the street. "Cassandra is now protected from vampires. They are unable to cross the town line."

Bernie was the town's wizened guru, the spiritual leader of the Cassandra community that worked closely with the mayor to run all aspects of the strange little psychic town. The mayor, by the way, is my boyfriend's mother—and, come to think of it, also my boss's girlfriend.

Small towns, right?

I don't know why anyone bothers to signal on the street. Everyone knows where everyone else is going, anyway.

Emma frowned. "If your town is protected from vampires and they can't come in, how is Ivy still here?"

"She's not fully transitioned," I reminded her. "Until she's a complete and total vampire, those wards won't affect her one way or another."

We chatted for a few more moments once again about Killian and why he might not have given us more information, speculating that maybe he was trying to protect Ivy in some way. But it was all just guesswork at this point.

We eventually said our goodbyes and parted ways. Emma and I rode silently for a bit, absorbed in our thoughts about the strange vampire ghost's afterlife insistence on saving the girl he was partially responsible for attacking.

"Do you think Killian is hiding something from us?" Emma asked as we drove back to Rex's bunker. "Well, I mean, obviously, he's hiding something from us. He won't answer questions. But is he not answering questions because he's focused on Ivy or because he's really trying to hide something?"

I thought for a moment.

I'd been focusing on Damien and Killian as a pair of nasty vampires, seeing them both as potential villains in whatever story we ultimately uncovered. Killian's death—and his insistence he wanted to help Ivy—wasn't very villain-like, though.

Rex claimed Killian was a bully, and I trusted Rex's take on things. Emma's brother had no reason to lie to us I could see, and he knew if he lied to Emma again, their relationship might not survive it.

If that was true, though, and Rex was right,

then why was Killian so focused on helping Ivy after all this time? Why did he refuse to turn Ivy, and why did he look so angry at Damien the night the sour vampire bit her?

"It's possible," I said, finally answering Emma's question. "But why would he do that? Do you think he's trying to protect Ivy in some way? He seems pretty focused on her for some reason, but I don't see any reason why he should be."

"General vampire regret? He likes her?" Emma mused. "But it's just a guess. We don't really know anything for sure."

"What about the Ambrogio?" Emma asked. "Do you think it has something to do with them?"

"In what way?"

"On the one hand, it makes sense that they would send an investigator, I guess—I mean, if they're the vampire government or whatever and Killian was their representative. That kind of thing sounds normal. If you know what I mean."

"It does," I agreed.

"But on the other hand," Emma continued, "it's possible that they're 'investigating Killian's death' because the information he won't tell us is somehow important to them—or important for them to keep hidden." Emma glanced at me. "Rudy said he'd been warned you were here,

Astra. At the time, I just thought it was because the two of you knew each other, but…" She nodded as though thinking to herself. "Killian sought out a witch that could communicate with him in the afterlife instead of going wherever other vampires go. If they—the Ambrogio—knew you were here in Forkbridge, they'd know your sister is here, your mother…and presumably, they know vampires have ghosts even if we didn't." She tapped the steering wheel. "Maybe they're worried he's going to talk."

I frowned, thinking about this. "That's a pretty big leap. Either way, I do think we need to be careful," I said. "If the Ambrogio is involved in Killian's murder, then this could be more dangerous than we thought."

"Not for us," Emma snorted. "If Rudy comes too close to me, Althea's vampire vitamin will bounce him like a basketball if he so much as thinks about messing up my hair."

"Vampires *can* still fire guns, you know."

"Oh." The detective sat up. "Well. Yeah. I guess I didn't think about that."

* * *

WE GOT BACK to Rex's bunker, and Emma questioned Rex vigorously—and a little confrontationally—about the Ambrogio. I, meanwhile, sat down with Ami and Jason, telling them everything we'd discovered that day.

Which, at first, seemed like a lot.

In the end, it didn't feel like much.

"So, what now?" Ami asked.

"I need you to do a reading about what's going on," I said, gesturing toward her tarot cards. "I need to know whether to chase in the direction of the Ambrogio and Rudy, this Adriana Kingsley vampire, or head back to Cassandra and demand Killian tell me what he's hiding."

Jason yawned next to me. Being underground all day with no sun and no fresh air clearly wasn't conducive to my boyfriend's normally high level of vim or vigor.

The first card that Ami flipped over was The Tower.

"This is about…a child," Ami said, pointing to the image of the small figure falling from the burning building. "All of it. The center of the whole situation is a child. I sense great… jealousy…yes, it's jealousy here around the child." Ami frowned and swayed on the chair slightly. "There is something…hidden that will soon be revealed, and it will be shocking or disturbing." Ami squinted. "And someone is in danger."

"Can you be more specific than that?" I asked.

She flipped over the next card, The Devil.

"This confirms what I said before," Ami said. "There is jealousy and envy at play here. But there is also a sense of manipulation and control. Someone is trying to control the situation because they don't want something known. Or do they know something they shouldn't? I can't really tell which it is."

"Can you tell who?" I asked.

She flipped over the next card, The Fool.

"This suggests that you are being careless," Ami said seriously without answering my question or giving me a single specific bit of information I could use. "You need to be careful, or you will make a mistake that could be costly."

I deploy my sister whenever I need a gut check—her gut on some things is far more developed than mine. I enlist her wisdom so often, it's practically an extension of my arm. But my sister's way of telling me I have no idea what I'm doing?

Annoying.

And wordy.

She flipped a card over and laid it across The

Fool. The Five of Swords. "What's hidden may not be what it seems right now."

Ami could not be more cryptic if she worked at it.

"Well, it doesn't seem like anything right now because we don't know what *it* is," Farah said, plopping down next to Ami. Damien and Rex walked over and stood behind my sister. The two vampires glanced down at the cards on the coffee table.

"Can you possibly be less general?" I asked Ami.

Her shoulders rose in a faint, helpless shrug. "I don't know this for sure, but...I think...I think Killian is the one keeping something hidden out of a sense of shame or isolation. He may feel like he can't tell anyone because they would judge him harshly. Whatever Killian is keeping hidden is something he is deeply struggling with," Ami told me, her eyes meeting mine. "This struggle's continued into his afterlife. It is not over yet."

"Oh, please," Damien sneered.

"Tell me more about this child," I asked, tapping The Tower. "Is this a baby, a young child, is someone pregnant? Is it Farah?"

"The hell it's me," she spat venomously. "I'm no child."

Ami frowned and shook her head. "I'm not sure," she said with a faint grimace. "All I can tell you is that the child is at the center of this whole situation. Whoever this child is, they are important to someone who wants to control them. Or...no. They are important to someone, and someone wants to control them. That might be two people." She looked up. "They may be in danger."

I looked up at Damien. "Is there anything you want to tell me?"

"Me?" His dark eyes, like those of a forest pool on the night of a new moon, reflected feigned innocence. His smile was wry, prompting me to believe nothing he said. Not even the one-word question. "I already sneered at it. It's bunk. A parlor trick for dimwits and humans that want to pretend—"

"Watch it," Jason warned him.

I laid a hand on Jason's arm. "Look, this all started with you," I told Damien with exasperation. "Like it or not, your life is in danger, and since your best buddy got whacked in the parking lot the same night your sparkle card turned over, my best guess says your possible imminent death has something to do with Killian's premature one."

"You think my best buddy got whacked because of me?" Damien asked with a raised eyebrow. "That's a bit of a stretch, don't you think? Is this how you people investigate? You just make up things until something sticks?" He looked at Emma. "No wonder your world is an absolute mess."

"I didn't say that Killian got whacked because of you," I responded. "But I do have to wonder why you just did."

Damien sighed and ran a hand through his dark hair. "You're right," he said, the sudden turnaround in his attitude giving me whiplash. "I guess I owe you an explanation."

I blinked.

That was…sudden.

"I'm all ears," I said, crossing my arms and leaning back against the chair.

The vampire stared at me for a long moment before finally speaking. "Killian and I were not as close as you seem to think we were," Damien began, his expression so sincere that I might have been speaking to a different vampire. My thoughts drifted down to the table and the cards that said this situation was rife with manipulation and control. "We were friends, but not close friends. We didn't share everything with each other."

It was like one day of sleep softened all the razor-sharp edges Damien Elkhart had used to verbally slice into anyone that got in his way.

"You pretended you owned Rex's club just because your friend Killian co-owned it. You and Killian lived in the same vampire nest in Atlanta. He followed you down here to Forkbridge." I ticked off all of the links between Damien and Killian I could recall off the top of my head. "Now, suddenly, you weren't that close?"

Emma stood to the side, observing. She'd grown periodically quiet since our conversation in the car on the way to Arden House, and it appeared to me that Killian wasn't the only one struggling with things in the midst of this case. I expected her to speak up in the silence that followed my question and Damien's lack of response.

But she didn't.

The silence stretched between us until it was broken by the sound of Rex's voice. "You guys were always close," he said quietly. "You may not have shared everything with each other, but you were still close friends. I saw. I'm not an idiot.

Damien," he said, his tone low and dangerous. "You need to tell us what's going on."

"Fine," Damien said, his voice tight with anger. "But I'm warning you, Rex, if you say anything about this to anyone else, I'll kill you myself."

"No, you won't," Emma warned him, her voice threateningly sinister.

* * *

DAMIEN'S STORY WAS...CREATIVE. I'll give him that.

He claimed that he and Killian were interested in buying some property on the outskirts of Forkbridge. I was familiar with the property—it was the old Thompson place, widely considered cursed and haunted.

It wasn't cursed, but it *was* haunted by Stephen Thompson.

And old Mr. Thompson, a ghost I knew from previous encounters through Ayla, wasn't about to let anyone buy his land.

Damien's story—told with a friendly smile that seemed so out of place I was sure someone had hit the vampire on the head while he was sleeping—was that the two vampires had handed over the money to buy the land for a new lair in Forkbridge, and they'd been duped. The property was not actually owned by the man who claimed to own it.

"So, you see, this has nothing to do with that girl in Cassandra, nothing to do with the Ambrogio, nothing to do with you people," Damien said, nodding. "Killian probably met with the man that stole our money, the man probably bought the Shroud Blade on the black market, and Killian wasn't prepared." His expression grew serious as he leaned against the couch. "Sad, terrible accident and all that, but Killian always was a bit overconfident."

"Does this man have a name?" I asked the vampire.

He shrugged. "What does it matter? He's probably long gone."

"Why couldn't you just tell us this last night?" Emma asked, her tone suspicious of Damien's words and his dramatic change in attitude. "This doesn't sound like some big conspiracy. In fact, it sounds like a run of the mill real estate scam."

"It's just so embarrassing."

"It's also absolute bunk," Jason said, speaking up for the first time all evening. "Can't you vampires read minds? Are you telling me two powerful, telepathic, paranormal beings got taken by a con man in a real estate scam?"

Damien looked startled and put a hand to his head. "Those vampire pills wear off at some point, do they?" The vampire's eyes narrowed.

"They do not." Jason stared back at Damien with a steady suspicion.

Rex, on the other hand, looked contemplative, as if he was thinking about Damien's story. Finally, he nodded as if he had come to a decision. "You don't really expect us to believe this, do you?" Rex inquired politely, glancing around the room.

"I expect you to remember where your loyalties lie." The implied threat in Damien's statement was clear to everyone in the room.

Rex stepped forward, but Jason jumped up and grabbed his shoulder.

Damien stepped toward Rex and Jason, trying to look intimidating.

"Oh, could you both stop it?" Farah said with irrepressible excitement as she placed herself between them without concern for the risk. (Though since I'd given her Althea's potion already, it's possible the spirited interruption was intended to provoke rather than derail the confrontation brewing.)

I ignored the vampires and turned back to Ami. "Is anything we've learned from him actually relevant to what's going on with the star card?" I asked her. "I'm with Rex, I suspect he just made up a story to shut us up, but I'd like some outside confirmation."

She grabbed all the cards laid out on the table, gathered them up, shuffled again, and flipped over a tarot card once more. "No," Ami said, her expression grim. "I don't know for sure that what he told us is a lie, but everything Damien said is irrelevant to the threat on his life—and Ivy's situation." Ami paused. "And Killian's death."

"You got all *that* from one card?" Damien asked with a biting arrogance.

"There he is," Farah said. She offered a gleeful grin to Damien. "And here I thought there might be a decent guy buried in there. Nope." She tapped a knife strapped to her waist, her delight evident. "I can't wait to gut you like a fish."

Damien arched an eyebrow as he looked her up and down. "You don't eat a lot of onions, do you? I hate onion-flavored blood." He turned back toward Ami. "I think you're just making this up. You can't get all that from one card."

"Well, obviously, we have to get it somewhere. We weren't going to get it from you. You're just going to stand there and lie to our faces." I told Damien, my voice tight with anger.

"You really expected us to believe this BS story about a real estate scam? Do you think we're idiots?"

"You really want me to answer that, or is that rhetorical?"

Rex stepped forward, his eyes narrowed into dangerous slits. "You need to remember who you're talking to, Damien," he demanded. "Astra is trying to help you. My sister is trying to help you. Everybody in this damn room is trying to help you."

"Not everybody. Not me," Farah deadpanned. "I'm just waiting until I can kill you." She pulled out her knife and waved it at him. "I doubt you're useful at all."

Damien flinched, shifting his gaze between Rex and me, Farah and Ami, and then back again. His fangs protruded from his mouth in a menacing manner, and his lips curled into a sneer. His pupils contracted, indicating his uncertainty, as his gaze darted to each of us.

Damien was well aware of the consequences of an attack.

I sensed he was debating whether he cared.

In the blink of an eye, Damien had morphed from the wolf who had run alongside us into a feral animal ready to swat anything that threatened him. The one thing you could count on with vampires.

Unpredictability.

I rolled my eyes. "Oh, stop with the—"

Wait.

Wait a minute.

Damien had dubbed the Ministry knife the *Shroud Blade,* as if it were some mythical Excalibur-like fantasy sword found during a quest.

And last night, Rudy had called it the same thing.

The Ministry, though, never named weapons like that.

Never.

To begin with, we never had a single magical weapon—if we could make one magical whacker, we could make a hundred of them, and we frequently did.

Second, names had power. A true name describes the essence of something, and the knowledge of that true name gives witches power over the person or thing that owns the name. That's why we always had multiples and stupid bureaucratic names and numbers for all our issued magical tools. We were warned repeatedly to never give them a nickname.

So, yeah.

The Ministry didn't name that blade.

"Damien, what do you know about this Shroud Blade?" Archie asked.

I looked at the owl, and he lifted his wings in a nonchalant gesture. Archie must have plucked my thoughts right out of my head. Which was…disconcerting.

The vampire slowly relaxed his stance. "What?"

"The Shroud Blade," Archie repeated. "What do you know about it?"

"I don't know anything about it," he stated defensively. "I overheard Rudy and Killian discussing it last night—" Damien stopped, his eyes wide.

"You heard *who* discussing *what*?" I asked.

The vampire slapped his hand over his mouth before jumping as his fang sliced into his finger. "Ow." He sucked on his bloody index finger and shrugged as casually as he could. "I mean, I thought I heard something in the club, but I didn't hear anything in the club," he said after pulling his finger from his mouth. Damien cast a glance at Rex. "The club was extremely loud. How could I possibly hear anything in the club?"

"You're really not good at this smooth

operator lying thing, are you?" Rex asked. "You're much better at brute force arrogance."

"Thank you," Damien said absentmindedly.

"What is it?" Emma asked, sensing my sudden change in mood.

I quickly outlined my realization about the name of the blade and why a witch would never have named it. "That would mean a vampire or the Ambrogio themselves are behind this after all," I said slowly, realization dawning on me. "They somehow got their hands on one of our weapons and named it. And now they're using it to kill vampires without being seen or caught by other vampires." I paused. "Maybe."

"Why does it have to be vampires?" Jason asked me.

"Because they both knew the name. Rudy and Damien."

"We need to go," Emma said, standing up. "We need to get back to Cassandra."

"Why?" Jason asked, looking confused.

"They have wards on the town," Archie explained. The owl rotated its head all the way around on its long, flexible neck until its unblinking eyes were fixated on my boyfriend. "If the vampires are killing people, we may all be in danger. The best way to protect that lying idiot may be to bring him behind the wards."

"But we literally can't do that because of the wards. Rex and Damien can't go," I pointed out. "They can't go into Cassandra."

Archie looked at me with bright, inquisitive eyes. "What do you think?"

"I think we're sitting in a VampB&B listed in a public vampire directory, and we need to change base camp."

CHAPTER ELEVEN

We fled Rex's bunker like our tails were on fire when it was dark enough for the vampires to travel. I'll admit that I wasn't convinced that the Ambrogio was to blame. The blade being named and Damien's little slip up that Rudy had been in Forkbridge while Killian was still alive were thin evidence, but it was enough for me to be wary of my old comrade.

And it was enough for us to run.

My mother was waiting for us in the entryway, her face lined with worry. "Archie said you were coming and would explain. What's going on?" she asked. "Why have you brought vampires here?"

I explained to her what we had learned about the (possible Ambrogio) knife and how we believed they could be behind Killian's murder. I told her we thought it was safest to stay here at Arden House until we could figure out what to do next.

She listened quietly, her face thoughtful. Finally, she nodded and said, "All right. We'll keep him safe here," my mother said as Damien blew past her toward the living room like he owned the place.

"I really dislike that vampire," I muttered.

"That being has some of the worst energy I've had the misfortune to be in the presence of. I wonder if I can make him eat some of the happy roses," Aunt Gwennie mused as she glanced across the hall toward the living room, referencing the antidepressant roses she grew in the front yard. "Though I doubt my happy roses would sweeten that sour disposition."

"I agree," my mother replied, her brow furrowed in worry. "I can absolutely understand why someone would want to kill the man." She sighed. "Unfortunately, it's better to be safe than sorry. We'll need to leave him as he is—we have no idea why Athena wants him alive. And if the Ambrogio is behind the threat to him, Astra, they won't rest until they find him. We need to be careful."

Aunt Gwennie turned to look at me. "You know, you can cast wards on places, Astra. It's not the most complicated spell ever. I'd be happy to teach you. You didn't have to come back here."

"Gwen, Astra has enough to worry about, what with her soldier running around Forkbridge and that girl in Cassandra that wants to turn back into a human." Mom dismissed the idea of me learning any magic that would prevent me from returning home in an emergency. "It's certainly easier for her to simply come back here."

It's also easier for Mom to keep her nose in my business.

"Yes, but there's nothing wrong with being prepared," Aunt Gwennie countered.

"Prepared for what?" Rex asked as he came out of the living room to join us. Emma trailed behind him. "Has something happened?"

"Nothing yet. But that's just it, Rex. Nothing has happened. But there's no way of knowing when it will." Gwennie's green eyes were scrunched up in frustration. "And I want to make sure that Astra is ready for whatever might happen."

"Oh, pish posh," Mom told her sister. "The covenstead is the safest place to be right now. Rex's bunker certainly wasn't the best idea."

Pish posh? "Everyone was fine there all day, Mom."

"I'm sure Astra and Emma can handle whatever comes their way." Rex put a hand on my mother's shoulders and smiled down at her. "Especially in this situation. I mean, look at how well Althea's potion works. It can tell the difference between malice and affection." Rex winked at my mom.

My mother rolled her eyes at the handsome vampire's flirtation. "Well, yes, that's very nice, dear," Mom admitted, "and speaking of your sister, have you heard from Althea or Ayla? Do you know how it's going in Cassandra?"

"We just left them a few hours ago, but no, I haven't checked in since then." I pulled out my phone and checked the text messages. "Nothing."

Mom nodded. "So, what's the next step?"

"The vampires are likely gathering at Sanguine," Rex replied. "Killian died there last night, the Ambrogio is in Forkbridge, so the most likely scenario is a meeting. The club is as close to a community center as we have." Rex glanced at Damien. "We can't take him, though."

"What do you mean *we*?" Emma asked, raising her eyebrow. "We can't take you, either. You can't take one of Althea's anti-vampire attack pills. I don't care if it is your club. You can't go with us. It's not safe."

"Because it is my club, I have to go," Rex answered. "If I don't show up, it'll look suspicious. The vampires will know something is wrong if I'm not there. I need to be there."

"No," Emma told her brother. "And the vampires know something is wrong, anyway. Killian Jarrow was killed. Rudy is here looking for clues. Clearly, the vampires already know something is wrong."

"I agree with Emma. You need to stay here, Rex." I set my jaw and jerked my chin up. "I mean it. I don't think she's being paranoid."

Aunt Gwennie leaned toward Emma. "Astra's right. We don't know anything yet, not for sure. The best thing we can do now is have someone, or multiple someones, go to the club and see what we can find out. Aunt Gertie has her hands full helping Ayla and Thea. Out of those free to go, I firmly believe we should only send people that are fully protected from vampires."

"Well, not fully. Vampires can shoot guns," Emma said.

We stared at her.

"Well, they can."

* * *

A BIT PAST NINE, we piled into Emma's car and headed toward Sanguine. Rex was not happy about staying at Arden House, but he did finally relent under the angry glare of his concerned sister.

"Is your owl coming with us?" Farah asked.

I pointed up.

"Huh. Cool. Anyway, Emma, your brother seems really nice," Farah said to the detective from the backseat. "I mean, for a vampire and all. He's cute, too. He reminds me of John Taylor from Duran Duran."

Emma laughed. "How do you know who that is? What are you, twelve?"

I glanced back. "And why would a vampire slayer actually like a vampire?"

"Would you stop calling me a vampire slayer?" she asked me with exasperated frustration. "I'm not a vampire slayer. I'm a vampire retributionist. That's totally different than a vampire slayer. First of all, a vampire slayer is fictional. There is no Hellmouth. I'm not from Sunnydale, and I sure as hell was never a cheerleader."

"Hey, slow down. That was a good show," I said to Emma.

"And she does have a crush on my brother, who's a vampire," Emma added, her lips forming into a hard line. "If there were a Hellmouth, it would no doubt be right in the middle of Forkbridge."

"You guys do have a pretty weird reputation," Farah agreed. "I mean, I'm from Savannah, and we have a reputation for ghosts and the like, but your reputation? It's even worse."

Emma frowned her eyes on the road.

I turned. "Our reputation with who?"

"Well, the vampire retributionists, for one. We have a private forum so we can trade information and keep up with what's going on all over the country. I mean, Sanguine? Okay, let me back up. Do you know how many vampire clubs there are in this country?"

I shook my head.

"Five. One in Las Vegas, one in Los Angeles, one in Chicago, and one in New York." She held out her fingers as she ticked off each one. "That's it. That's the entire nation. And then there's you, a big vampire club in a tiny town in Central Florida. One of these things is not like the other."

"Huh." I didn't know that.

"And none of them have the kind of reputation that the Forkbridge Sanguine has, either. Even the ones in the big cities."

"What kind of reputation is that?" Emma asked.

"So, some history. The New York Sanguine was the first vampire club. It got started during the Great Depression. The head vampire, Alistair, he started the first vampire club, and then he kept it going through the worst of the Great Depression. He gave jobs to people who couldn't find work anywhere else, and he kept the clubs open when no one else could."

"So he's a vampire philanthropist," I supplied. "Interesting."

"Exactly. And his club is reputable. Everyone knows it." Farah nodded. "It's not a place that a retri would go, even if she was a retri. Retributionists don't associate with vampires, right? We kill them. We watch them. We punish them. We're not going to hang out with them and party. Anyway, the other four were modeled after New York. They're not the same, obviously, but they're modeled after that one."

"But not Sanguine," I guessed.

"Well, sort of. The Forkbridge Sanguine has a reputation of being…well, it's a pretty wild place." She thought for a moment. "Well, wilder than the other four, anyway. It's mostly on the back of this one vampire. He's a new vampire, really, but he's been at the club a lot. He's tall but kind of not in good shape. He's got this long, lazy face like he's constantly amused, but he's not. He's just kind of creepy."

I wasn't sure who she was talking about. Nothing in her decryption was ringing a bell. "Creepier than normal vampire creepy?" I asked.

Farah nodded. "And he's never had any trouble killing a vampire retributionist. He doesn't talk about it. Doesn't brag about it. He just does it. And he does it in a very creative way. He doesn't just kill them. He makes sure that they're humiliated when they die. He does it in a way that no one will ever know how they were killed. It looks like an accident. No suspicion." She paused. "But he makes sure *we* know. Anyway, you guys are kind of notorious. Oh, and Rex has a reputation of being a womanizer."

"I had no idea. You guys know a lot about vampire gossip, huh?" Emma said as she pulled into the parking lot.

"Wait, back up," I said to Farah. "You said this guy was new. How new?"

Farah shrugged. "I don't know for sure. Maybe six months or so. He supposedly doesn't talk about it, but one of the other retris said that he was a new vampire."

"Does he have a name?"

"Delaney."

CHAPTER TWELVE

Why Morticia and Twinkle let us into the club, I had no idea. The place was packed with vampires, and we appeared to be the only creatures not undead.

They were all dressed to the nines, too.

Some were in historical costumes, and others were in clothes right out of western films. Each group had a proprietary style, a look clearly their own.

Now I knew why Farah had been worried about finding Delaney—there were so many vampires in the place she might as well have been looking for a specific snowflake among all those tossed on a blustery day.

We had just passed through the front entrance of the club, which was mostly wide open, to the atrium and kitchens beyond. The walls were covered in vines and flowers, making it look like we were inside a greenhouse. The lights were dimmed way down low and cast a soft, warm glow over everything.

Rudy Redmond stepped into our path.

Rudy considered me with a raised eyebrow and crossed his arms. "What are you doing here?" His black leather outfit creaked as he leaned his back against the wall. "I'm not sure if you've noticed, but there are no humans here. No witches. Just vampires."

"Hi, Rudy."

"You just can't keep your nose out of things that don't concern you, Arden," he said. "Just like the old days, huh?" The old days with Rudy, when we were still learning our way around the paranormal world. Before he'd been turned. Before I'd left him in Egypt. "A little cooler, though. But not by much."

"Everything in this town concerns me. A vampire being killed at this club concerns me. A vampire being killed with a knife stamped with a Ministry inventory number concerns me even more."

"Where is it?" he asked casually.

"Where's what?"

"The blade."

"The Shroud Blade, you mean?"

"What else would I mean?" Rudy sighed. "You know that it's a murder weapon. You can't keep evidence. I need to examine it."

I wondered if it would help to tell Rudy that the blade was in Arden House, that I'd made sure it was kept behind vampire wards so he couldn't get it. But I didn't want him to know that I had left it in the hands of my family. Wards or not, I didn't trust Rudy Redmond.

"Last I checked, you're not a cop. I just thought I'd hang on to it a little while longer. I promise I'll turn it over as soon as I have a chance to have it fingerprinted," I lied.

"Turn it over to who?"

I didn't answer.

Rudy shook his head, a disappointed expression on his face. "I've given you nothing but respect, Arden. I thought you were a sensible woman. It looks like I was wrong."

"What's that supposed to mean?"

"It means that you're stepping on a lot of toes, making a lot of enemies. You need to back off." Rudy shrugged, but he was nervous. I could see it in the way he shifted his weight and the way he wouldn't meet my eyes.

"Who's toes? What enemies?" I wanted to remind him he wasn't the boss of me, but it seemed a petty, childish thing to say. "You don't know anything about me or my family. You have no right to be giving me orders, and you're especially not going to do it in my town."

"I'm not giving you any orders. I'm just advising you to do what's best for you." Rudy's tone was suddenly cold and threatening. "Killian's death has nothing to do with you. Nothing."

"Thanks for the advice. If I need it, I'll keep it in mind."

Rudy sighed with abject frustration. "Look, I'm not trying to be a jerk here, okay? You don't have to cooperate, but it will make this much more pleasant for you if you do. I'm trying to be reasonable here. I really am. But you can be awfully difficult." He leaned against the cold stone wall, leaning in to whisper with a dark grin, "I can't force you to cooperate. But I can make things very uncomfortable for you."

"I'm shaking in my boots," I said sarcastically.

Rudy glanced over Emma and Farah, a condescending expression on his face. "Your friends might be." He pushed away from the wall. "Look, I already have enough problems. I don't need you adding to them. Stay out of my way."

* * *

IT DIDN'T TAKE LONG for things to get interesting.

"Thank you so much for coming, all of you," a female vampire said from the stage. She was taller than me, and thin—with a little bit of wiggle to her. She wore a pink silk blouse and a black velvet skirt with a simple but elegant necklace. Her eyes were an ocean blue, her skin pale, her hair pale blond and straight. She stood tall and beautiful, her manner poised and confident.

She also looked exactly like the woman in Ivy's vision.

The mysterious Adriana Kingsley.

"Killian Jarrow was a well-respected vampire. Despite his young age, he embraced the Ambrogio lifestyle with both cold hands, serving the community of Forkbridge with a blood lust for true justice and a deep concern for order." Adriana's voice was strong and compelling. "For this, he has earned the respect of all his patrons at the Ambrogio. He was a true gentleman."

"True justice," the crowd chanted, saluting Killian's picture.

Adriana's high heels clicked as she moved across the floor. Her words echoed in the silent room like an off-key piano in an empty concert hall. Everyone turned their heads to stare at her, their faces a collection of shock and horror.

"Normally, when a vampire dies, there's a period of sorrow and mourning," Adriana continued. "Time is taken to remember the dead vampire's life, to give thanks for the good he or she did. But tonight isn't normal. Tonight, we are mourning not just one vampire, but the Ambrogio representative here in Forkbridge. He had so much potential as a leader. Such a shame."

"Shame," the crowd chanted in response.

"It's a terrible shame this potential was cut short by a senseless murder." She paused, her gaze moving over the room. "And that this crime has yet to be solved."

A restless murmur washed over the crowd. I surveyed the sea of faces, trying to find Rudy. Finally, I spotted him leaning against the bar alone, smoking a cigarette. A wicked sneer broke out on his face when he looked at the stage, and then an instant later, it was gone.

Emma noticed me staring at him, grabbed my arm, and closed her eyes, her face solemn. Images from our connection flashed quickly in my mind, then slowed. Finally, a clear scene—Rudy was leaning over to speak to a tall, lanky vampire to the stage's right. A vampire I'd never seen before.

"Got it," I whispered, releasing her hand.

Several vampires turned and stared, and I realized why we'd been let into the club. Every vampire in this place could hear every whisper as loudly as if we'd shouted the words through the PA system. Emma's already realized this; that's why she'd grabbed my hand and silently shared what she'd seen with me.

"Many of you have come forward with information. Thank you for your time and your candor." Adriana's eyes skimmed over the crowd. "But there are still those of you with information who have not shared it with the Ambrogio investigator."

There was a collective gasp from the crowd.

"To encourage you, we have a special guest of honor tonight," Adriana continued, her voice infused with a hint of excitement. "The Ambrogio Administrator herself, Lila Redmond. I'm sure you're all eager to impress her. In the meantime, I think we all understand the importance of sharing information with the Ambrogio."

"Are you kidding me? Who wants to die next, right?" a voice shouted from the back of the crowd. "If any of you talk to her, you're a moron."

Well.

Not everyone was a fan of the Ambrogio.

"You're not supposed to speak unless asked a direct question, moron," a vampire shouted.

"See how you like it when she stabs you," the rebellious vampire hissed.

"Let me make this perfectly clear." Adriana's strong voice filled the room. "If you know anything about this crime, especially if you might know something that could identify the murderer, you must come forward. It is your duty."

"Or what?" I whispered to Emma.

"Or you will be dealt with accordingly," Adriana said, her voice echoing across the room. She paused, the silence heavy. "I will tolerate no more secrets. This was no random murder. Someone here knows. Someone here may even be responsible."

At that, Lila Redmond stood up.

She was as tall as Adriana, but unlike Adriana,

Lila exuded power. This was a woman who did not shy away from making difficult decisions, but rather welcomed the challenge. Her hair was pulled back in a tight bun, and she was dressed sternly in a black gown that made her lips look like a scarlet slash. She rested her hand on her hips. "Anyone that has information and withholds it will face the ultimate punishment," Lila said quietly.

After delivering that one sentence, she immediately stepped down.

"Ambrogio Administrator Lila Redmond," the crowd chanted, saluting her with their drinks.

"That was a mouthful. Not very talkative, is she?" Emma whispered.

A vampire in front of Emma turned to stare at her. His eyes blazed with anger as he glared at the human who dared to speak so of the Administrator.

"Sorry," Emma said with a nod.

Adriana returned to her previous place, center stage. "You know what happened, and you know what it means. If you've been holding back because you're afraid, we are here to tell you that we don't have time for fear. We must find the killer and bring them to justice. Forkbridge must not be tainted with violence." She turned to leave but paused. "I'm not asking you to come forward. I'm demanding it."

* * *

"So, how do we do this when all the vampires can hear what we say?" Farah asked as the three of us sat down at a booth near the back of the club.

"Do what?" I looked up to find the angelic-looking Adriana Kingsly staring down at us. "What did a witch, a vampire hunter—"

"Retributionist," Farah corrected.

"—and a human detective come to this club to do, exactly?"

"We're here to hear what you have to say," I said with a smile, trying to look harmless. "We heard your speech, and we thought we could help."

"Help?" She raised one eyebrow. "We don't need your help. The Ambrogio representative was my business partner. This is a personal issue for me. I have it well under control."

He was more than that, but I noticed she didn't mention their personal relationship, not in her speech and not to us.

"I was the one who found him. This is my

town. This is her brother's club," I said, pointing toward Emma. "It's personal for me, too."

"We want to talk to you," Emma said, staring straight into her eyes.

"No. I'm afraid I don't have any questions for you." She smiled, her eyes slightly narrowed. "I have everything I need to know about you. I can pluck it all right out of your minds. You're like helpless children, with all your thoughts laid open."

But that wasn't true, not at all.

At least not with the three of us.

Althea's defensive vampire vitamins defended our minds from being forcefully probed by vampires. Adriana could see what we showed her, but nothing that we protected from her.

She either didn't know that or lied about her capabilities.

"Is that a threat?" I asked, getting to my feet.

"I have no desire to threaten you. I have no reason to." She shrugged. "But I'm also not about to sit here and let you interrogate me. Good evening, Detective." She turned to leave. "Witch." She ignored Farah like she wasn't even there.

"Wait," I said quickly, touching her arm.

She looked down at my hand, her face turning to ice. I pulled my arm away.

"Please," I said quickly, forcing a pleading tone that might make the woman feel more powerful. "We're on the same side here. We just want to help find who murdered Killian."

"Then I'm afraid you're wasting your time with me."

Farah shuddered, and I glanced over to find her staring at Adriana, her face contorted in disgust, watching the vampire walk away.

"What?" I asked.

"Do you notice the way she walks?" Farah said slowly. "She's not even putting any weight on her feet, but she's still moving so fast. She's like a machine, but with a personality. I don't think she even cares that you're here. She's all about appearances and appearances alone."

Adriana glared back toward Farah.

I took out the small obsidian rock I carried with me everywhere. I activated it by slamming it into the center of the table. The blackened stone exploded into a rainbow-colored bubble that engulfed our table and its occupants. As the music faded to silence, the vampires stared. "Okay, they can't hear anything we say," I told Farah and Emma. "What do we think?"

"I don't remember anyone claiming Adriana was Ambrogio. How did she become the leader of this little Ambrogio memorial interrogation party thing?" Emma asked us. "And just as a random point—that woman makes my skin crawl."

"Well, it's obvious that she wanted us in here, and she wanted us to see that. Otherwise, the Gothic twins at the front door never would have let us in," I pointed out. "And Lila Redmond? Is that Rudy's wife?" I looked back and forth between Emma and Farah. "Do vampires get married like normal people?"

"What the hell are you asking us for?" Farah said with an eyebrow raise. "Weren't you the one that lived in Impy City for fifteen years, training in paranormal whatever?"

"That paranormal whatever was how to capture and kill paranormals, Farah. I didn't take a sociology class to learn about other species."

"We're getting off track. Who cares if they're married," Emma said, looking from Farah to me. "Do you think she did it?"

"I don't know," Farah said. "I'm mostly just annoyed by her attitude. She seems capable, though."

"They're all capable. They're vampires. What do you think?" I asked Emma and Farah.

"I don't know," Emma said. "Yes, she's capable, but I can't tell if she did it or not. And I still have no idea why she would—though this whole thing tonight was pretty weird. Why hide their relationship?"

"Me neither," Farah said. "But we need to find out more about her. We know the least about her, and that makes her the most suspicious." Farah looked at me. "So, how do we find out more about her?"

CHAPTER THIRTEEN

*H*e wrapped his talons around my hair and pulled my head toward his beak. "It's obvious," he said, his voice coming out high-pitched and squawky. I pulled my hair from his grasp. "I mean, it's so obvious. I can't even understand why you came out here to talk to me. The answer is right in front of you. Right in front of you." The bird shook his head. "Right in front of your face, Astra."

"I'm sorry, Archie, but I have no idea what you're talking about."

"We've been wasting time going to vampire gatherings and walking right into these places. Emma and Farah are in Sanguine right now, and everyone there knows they are there. So they won't hear anything." Archie tapped the steering column with his claw. "It's all a total mess, Astra. Everything is a game. And we need to start playing smarter."

"Don't do that. What game?"

The owl perched on the dashboard, his eyes wide. "The game they're playing. The vampires."

I held up my hand. "Hang on. I don't have time for *your* games. Speak plainly here, please, and tell me exactly what you mean."

"Whoooooo's playing a game?" Blink.

"Archie, what is wrong with you?"

"Besides the vampires, I mean." The owl bobbed his head up and down. "They want everyone to think they don't know what's going on. That they're not saying anything. That they don't know anything. But they're probably communicating all over the place, and we can't hear them! Because they know. They know! It's so obvious to me." He grabbed one of his feathers, yanked it, and threw it down. "Why can't you see it?"

My bird had lost his mind.

"Look." I tried to speak in a calming voice. "The only thing right in front of me is that I'm losing my patience, and you're acting like a nutcase."

"I crack nut cases for breakfast! You're losing your patience? That cuts like a *knife*." The owl squawked, his voice sounding like it was blowing out a speaker. "I'm supposed to be helping you to be better. So be better. You're not the sharpest *knife* in the drawer tonight." He flapped his wings and hopped from the dash to the passenger seat. "I gave you the answer. You just don't see it. I bet you're on a *knife's edge* of figuring it out, though."

I wasn't sure if the bird was drunk, on drugs, or just in one of his moods, but I did finally get what he was saying. Since he, you know, finally said it.

Sort of.

"You want me to use the blade," I said. "Which I am totally willing to discuss with you. But why not just say that? What is with all this ranting and raving?"

"Like I said, I'm supposed to be helping you get better. You know, to think for yourself." He rubbed his feathered head. "It also could be that I got hungry while watching the parking lot and grabbed a snack. Someone dropped a bag of jelly beans, and I ate them. All of them. Well, not the black ones. I don't even know why they exist. But I ate all the other colors." He fluffed up his feathers and looked away, pecking them with his beak. "It's a lot of sugar. A lot of sugar. I'm a little hopped up on sugar." He paused. "Okay, maybe a lot hopped up." He paused. "On sugar."

"Don't take this the wrong way," I told the owl, "but you're freaking me out."

"My customary diet is almost entirely devoid of glucose, so this stuff's hitting me like a...like a... anyway, wait. Check this out. If you want to get freaked out, witch girl, watch this." The owl wretched up a multicolored pellet of brown fur wrapped around a half-digested rainbow of jelly beans, skittles, red vines, and other candies right onto my leather seats. "Huh. Look at that. I forgot about the skittles."

"Oh my God." I tried to clean up the mess. Archie just sat there, his innocent expression passive, his feathered wings motionless as he watched me. "Thanks so much, by the way," I said as I took another napkin to wipe up the mess.

"You're welcome." He blinked. "For what?"

"That was sarcasm. Do you not have sarcasm on Mount Olympus or wherever you were kept for thousands of years before they decided you'd be the perfect companion for me? I mean, you have to, right? Lord knows you barely have the ability to speak without using it."

"I know, I—" Archie stopped, stared at me, and blinked again. "Wait. That was sarcasm."

"You realize that since I've met you, I've been threatened, attacked, threatened some more, attacked some more, and now you've just vomited an owl pellet covered in jelly beans and skittles on my leather seats." I tossed the dirty napkin into the Jeep's tiny trash bag. "And this is all *after* I left the military."

He fluffed up his feathers again.

"No comment?"

"Anyway," Archie said with a huff. "Use the blade. You were wearing gloves the other night when you grabbed it. I think Damien and Rex wouldn't have been able to see you if you'd had the gloves off."

I frowned. "You think?"

"Magic targeting a person or desire is complicated," he said. "That's why Althea's vampire pill is such a marvel. That girl…anyway, it's wrapped up in intentions, individual intentions. The Ministry couldn't create a blade that would adjust to different vampires and different scenarios that would suit all of you. My guess is that knife—the one that caused Killian to see a disembodied weapon headed for him but not the hand that held it?"

"I know which one you're talking about—"

"That knife—"

"Makes whoever—"

"Exactly, but don't say it," Archie nodded, glancing toward Sanguine. "They might be able to hear you. Anyway, it may be time for you to read that knife. And if you can't read it—"

"And I probably can't. The Ministry made tools unreadable by default."

"—then it may be time to use it so we can find out what's really going on with these vampires." The owl bobbed his head up and down. "But one way or another, you're going to find out what's going on. They're certainly not going to tell us, and they'll see us coming from a mile away."

* * *

FOR THE RECORD, I did not want to use the blade. The idea that the blade could magically conceal the knife-wielder from any vampire, regardless of how well they knew the person wielding the blade, made me uneasy. It's just one of those things that I don't believe should have ever been invented.

The situation had changed, though.

I wanted to get my hands on the knife again after discovering (or rather, realizing) that it rendered its user invisible to all vampires. I really wanted to infiltrate wherever the Ambrogio were hiding out and figure out what was going on. The situation was getting ridiculously convoluted, and more vamps were showing up in Forkbridge every day.

I headed back into the club, grabbed Emma and Farah, and pulled them into the parking lot. "We need to head home. I have to get something," I said, not wanting to discuss the plan until we were well away from super-powered ears. Like everything else I had stashed away for safety—namely, Damien and Rex—the knife was back at Arden House in the care of my mother and Aunt Gwennie.

The sidewalks were empty. No one walked the streets in this neighborhood except for club-goers and cops. I tried to ignore the feeling that lurked in my chest as we weaved in and out of the streets, but after three blocks, I realized a dark sedan weaving behind us was—possibly—on our tail.

So I tested the theory.

Sure enough, when I sped up, the car behind me did, too. I made a left turn, and it turned as well, rolling through the stop sign to stay close. I took a right, and it did the same.

"Well, that's...odd," Emma murmured, noticing it, too.

I put my foot on the brake as we slowed for a red light, and the car behind me drove up close —slamming on the breaks just inches away from my extra off-road tire. "What the heck, dude?" I muttered, straining to make out who was in the vehicle. I couldn't see the driver, but I thought I could see the silhouette of a passenger, as well as two very large men in the back seat. "They're not jumping out," I whispered. "That's a good sign."

"But they're not backing off, either," Farah pointed out.

I accelerated again and made another right turn, then another, heading toward a more populated area with streetlights and houses.

The car stayed with me.

Farah's voice sounded behind me. "Is there a way to lose them?"

"I'm trying." I turned down a long, dark street and slammed on the accelerator, pointing the Jeep toward a dirt road behind the housing development. "I doubt that sedan has off-road capabilities."

"We should have brought my car," Emma complained. "This would have been over already."

"Yes, yes, you're so much faster than me." Emma's disparagement of the Jeep's speed caused me to pound my foot on the gas pedal. The Jeep bounced and fishtailed wildly as we jumped the curb and took off over the uneven ground.

The sedan had also made its way onto the dirt road, but it was struggling to keep up. The lights in my rearview mirror grew smaller.

"Take that, sedan," I muttered with a glare.

"Astra!" Farah shouted, her voice frantic. "Watch out for that puddle! It's huge. It might be deep. You need to slow down. We'll get stuck!"

I smiled.

"Oh, great. Now you've done it," Emma sighed.

"I've done what?" Farah squealed. "What did I do?"

"Hang on!"

As our front-end lurched a foot into the muddy water, Farah and Emma yelped, reaching for the grab bar handles (commonly known as the "Oh, poo" handles, though the word for poo used was somewhat less refined and a bit more feisty).

"Astra, be careful!" Emma warned.

"We're fine," I responded calmly.

The Jeep rocked violently as it clawed its way through the muddy, wet muck toward the other side. We slowed to a crawl as we crossed, but with my oversized pizza cutter tires, we easily made it to the other side of the ten-foot water-filled ditch.

I came to a halt once we were back on solid ground and returned my gaze to the sedan through my rearview mirror.

They were confident.

I'll give them that.

Until the last second, when they hit the brakes a little too hard, they were confident they could take the puddle with a little speed and creative driving.

They were wrong.

The sedan swerved as its tires lost traction on the muddy road, sending it sideways. The car skidded into the standing water, which, judging by the driver's surprised expression, was larger and deeper than he had anticipated.

Honest to goddess, it was like a scene from a cartoon.

"They won't drown, will they?" Farah asked, concerned.

"Nope. They didn't flip, so they'll be fine." I paused. "Wet and muddy, but fine. They might lose their shoes, though, if they try to get out. Mud like that has a way of ripping those things right off your feet."

"They could make it across," Emma pointed out. "They're still moving."

I laughed out loud. "You wanna bet me?"

Emma wisely didn't respond.

There wasn't much the driver of the sedan could do. The tires spun in the mud, sending a spray of brown muck up. The sedan wobbled as it inched through the mud and slowly came to a halt, the engine roaring as whoever was inside tried to break free and move forward through sheer force of power—power that was actually digging his car in deeper.

Water poured from the roof and cascaded down the windows in thick rivulets. The engine finally shut down, the car stopped sinking, and the driver got out.

"Uh oh," Farah whispered.

"What the hell is wrong with you?" Muddy McSunken demanded with a shout.

I chuckled and got out. "Nothing wrong with me," I shouted back. "My Jeep made it through that just fine. Looks to me like you're the one having a problem, friend."

He stood over six feet tall. He had a lean body,

broad shoulders, and a well-kept silver beard that flowed nearly down to his chest. He walked toward me, water slapping and mud sucking at his boots, his expression a mix of irritation and annoyance. "What did you think you were doing?"

"Saving my life? Protecting my friends?" I asked innocently. "I mean, you really can't blame me for trying to get away. You see," I waved at the woods behind me, "out here in the country, the wildlife can be a bit dangerous. When something sneaks up on you all quiet-like, you assume it's trouble." I narrowed my eyes and tensed. "And you, friend, have gotten close enough. Why were you following me?"

"Why were you running?" the man asked, his voice stiff. He trudged through the mud like a Spartan at Thermopylae, face set against the elements to conquer his foes.

"That's not an answer," I snapped. "I'll ask you one more time, and I will ask you again not to come an inch closer. Why were you following me? Think really, really long and hard about whether you want to answer that question with a question. I'm the one with a Jeep and recovery gear, and you're the one with a sedan stuck in a mud bog."

He stomped his feet as he made it to solid ground, stopped, and twisted to look at his watch. "Fine. I was asked to check on you," the man replied. "We were worried about you." His biceps bulged as he heaved his muck-caked boot from the sucking, smelly mud and stomped again.

"We? Who's we?"

The silver-haired man looked at me, and within seconds, his eyes changed to a deep, velvety brown as silvery gray fur began to grow down his muscled arms. His face and teeth elongated, forming the head of a gray wolf. The wolf crouched before me for a moment, and I could swear its wolfy expression was etched into a frown.

"You must be kidding." I glared hard at the wolf as he shifted back into a human. They do this with such ease they tend to forget that when they shift back, they're super naked. His bare chest glistened with a sheen of sweat, and I tried to keep my eyes firmly on the muddy wolf's face.

He held up his hands, his eyes still brown. "I swear by the moon, we were worried—"

"Yeah, before we have a chat, could you do me a favor and cover that up, please?" I asked, pointing vaguely toward the werewolf's exposed bits. "There could be children looking out a window somewhere. No one needs to see that."

He cracked a half-smile. "We're in the middle of the—"

"Clothes! Please!"

The werewolf sighed. "Just a moment." His body shifted, growing and elongating as his jaw elongated into a muzzle. This time, black hair covered his body until he was covered in a thick pelt. Before he fully became a wolf, he shifted back into human form, and his clothes—now all black—miraculously reappeared on his body.

"That's a pretty good trick," I said. "I'm wondering, though, why you didn't just do that at the beginning. I have a boyfriend, so no use hitting on me."

"I don't!" Farah announced as she climbed out of the Jeep's back seat. "I am totally single! How're you doing? My name's—"

"Are you Emma Sullivan?" the werewolf asked. The men behind him finally emerged from the bog and stood silently behind him. It was as if the silver-haired man was the leader of this group.

Er, pack.

Whatever.

"No, my name's Farah, and you're incredible

looking!" she breathed. "I've never seen a real werewolf in the flesh before. Or fur, I guess?" She pulled her phone out. "You mind if I get a selfie?"

"Remember your big speech about how you're not a child?" I inquired of her. "Yeah, go over what you just said really carefully in your mind, and think about it for a minute." I returned my attention to the silver wolf. "How did you meet Emma?"

"You're Astra, the goddess-chosen witch, yes? You match the description we were given, though we were told you would be in a Ministry uniform."

"You know more about me than I know about you, friend," I said, crossing my arms again. "That's starting to annoy me. Again, what do you want?"

"We were sent here to help if we can," the man said, holding his hands out in a placating gesture. "I'm sorry, but we don't have time to explain everything to you. This area is not very defensible." He glanced at Farah one more time, then back to me. "Eddie Renzo feared Emma's life could be in danger because of the vampire situation here. If you're her friend, we're asking you to help us. Tell us where she is so we can honor our pack mate's request."

That explains why the silver wolf resembled a wealthy silver fox.

Detective Eddie Renzo was Emma's friend. They'd both served in the regular human military, though she had no idea he was a werewolf until we got to Palm Beach. He felt more at ease coming out to Emma after discovering she had a witch—me—for a best friend. She handled the revelation admirably.

Okay, not at first.

"Don't any of you people just use phones?" I asked with some exasperation.

The Jeep passenger door opened, and Emma emerged, a curious expression on her face. "I am Emma. Who are you, and what's the code word?"

"My name is Wyatt Marlow. That's Lawrence Roselin, Norden Morris, and Lothian Pennington. We are from the Palm Beach wolf pack."

"What's the real name of this pack?" I asked.

Wyatt looked at me. "What's the true name of your coven?"

It was worth a shot.

"The codeword is Brezgigeod."

"Eddie sent him," Emma said with a nod. "We set up a code word to use if we ever had to send someone instead of coming ourselves. Good to meet you, Wyatt."

"Likewise, Emma." Wyatt bowed as he spoke, and I was reminded of a courtier's attitude toward their monarch. "My alpha hopes you'll forgive our lack of foresight. When we realized we had not been invited to the gathering, we decided to come anyway. Especially after Eddie grew concerned for you. He recalled your brother might be at the center of all this drama, which would likely put you near the center as well."

"Yeah, Eddie knows me. Thank you," Emma said, giving Wyatt a little salute. "Wait. What gathering?"

Wyatt gave her a shocked look. "The Ambrogio Ascension?"

Emma cocked her head to one side, her expression a mix of curiosity and disbelief. "The what?"

CHAPTER FOURTEEN

"Are you all right?" Jason Bishop, my patient and long-suffering boyfriend, greeted me at the door of Arden House. His handsome face was full of concern as the three of us, muddy and sweaty, traipsed into the house with three large men in tow. Lothian, the fourth werewolf, stayed out front with their damaged car.

"Werewolves," I said, gesturing behind me. "Emma's friend Eddie Renzo asked some of his pack mates to head up here. They say there's something called an Ambrogio Ascension happening here in Forkbridge. Before you ask, no idea what that is."

"An Ambrogio Ascension…" Jason murmured.

He was wearing Aunt Gwennie's dainty chef's apron, and I could smell the fresh bread in the air. My stomach rumbled. Jason had a way of toasting slices of freshly baked French bread and sprinkling them with herbs and vegetables that made my mouth water. "Is it some sort of religious thing?"

"It is an ancient custom that is said to have originated with the Ambrogio clan eons ago," Wyatt said. "They think it opens up a way to talk to their goddess, Athena."

My head snapped up. "Whoa. Hold up. Athena? Are you sure it's Athena?"

"Artemis? Alethea? I don't know. One of the A-named Greek goddesses."

"It's Artemis, Wyatt," Lawrence Roselin said quietly from behind him. "The Ambrogio vampires follow Artemis. Or, well, they don't follow her, but they think she holds them in special esteem."

"I didn't pay a lot of attention in that class," Wyatt admitted.

My mother peeked around the corner, her eyes dancing with delight. "Werewolves have a class on the gods?" she asked, her voice rising in surprise. "I'm impressed."

"Um, no, ma'am. I took a mythology class at

Harvard," Wyatt responded.

Mom couldn't hide her disappointment.

"Artemis was a goddess of the hunt and of the moon," Emma said. "I think she's been called Diana in some circles, maybe, but Artemis was her original name."

The wolves stared at Emma as if she was giving a lecture at Harvard, waiting patiently for her to go on.

She cleared her throat. "If I remember correctly, Artemis was the Greek goddess of the hunt and the moon and was a virgin. She never had any interest in men and, according to most accounts, never took a lover and never married."

My mother beamed, her disappointment in Wyatt eclipsed by her pride in Emma. "Very good, dear."

"I'm sorry," Wyatt said. "I don't follow all the religious stuff."

"That's fine," my mother told him. "A leaf doesn't need to believe in photosynthesis for it to turn green, dear."

Wyatt looked confused. "I don't know what that means."

"Hey, I do have a question. Why didn't Eddie show up himself?" I asked Wyatt. He seemed to be in charge and the only werewolf who appeared to talk a lot. "How come he sent you guys instead?"

I noticed the three men all exchanged uncomfortable glances.

"It's really not our place to explain why Eddie sent us instead of coming himself," the one named Norden responded softly. "But if you truly have a need to know this information, Ms. Sullivan should be able to—"

"Too much," Wyatt barked at Norden. "Don't say anymore."

The men said nothing else, but their gazes darted back and forth from me to Emma (who looked a little uncomfortable suddenly,.)

"Okay," I said. "That wasn't weird at all."

Everyone, now—my mother, Jason, me, Farah, as well as the werewolves and Archie—glanced around, trying to understand why the dragged-on silence suddenly felt so heavy—but no one was more bewildered than me as I watched Norden, Lawrence, and Wyatt all press their lips together like they were trying to swallow a secret.

"Ms. Sullivan?" I asked, my eyebrow raised. "You have something you want to share with the class?"

Emma looked like she might throw up. "No."

"Well, shoot, now *I* want to know," Jason said.

"Weird things have a way of turning into bad things. What's going on?"

"It's nothing you all need to be concerned about. Suffice it to say that Eddie Renzo is with child," Norden said. "Our alpha and his mate have recently conceived."

"Your alpha?" Jason asked.

"And *his* mate?" my mother asked slowly, her eyes drifting toward Emma.

"Stop it," Wyatt said, growling.

"That's great for them, I guess," I said, slightly confused. "Congratulations?"

"Thank you," Norden said. "We are grateful for your good wishes."

My mother's eyes thoughtfully drifted back and forth between Emma and the wolves. "Oh my goodness." Her face was soft, her smile etched with concern. "Oh, child," she whispered to Emma. "Is this not good news?"

"Is what not good news?" I asked my mother with a confused look on my face. "What news are you talking about? Did I miss something?"

"Right in front of her face," Archie muttered from the corner. "Does she see it? Nope. Right there. So close, it might bite her."

"Archie," Mom scolded gently and then nodded her head. She stepped forward, and though I was watching Emma turn seven shades of red, I caught the movement out of the corner of my eye. I turned to look at Mom, and she touched me on the shoulder. "I think your friend has been avoiding certain conversations with you, Astra," she said softly.

"Oh, for heaven's sake, this is starting to feel like a soap opera episode. I'm pregnant," Emma said, her face pale. "Okay? No big deal. There. Everyone knows."

"You can't be," I responded like an idiot. "You're not seeing anyone."

I don't know why I didn't see what was going on.

It was obvious, at that moment, that Emma had been seeing someone—Eddie Renzo. It wasn't a surprise, really, that they'd be romantically involved. I could sense the deep respect and care between them when we went to Palm Beach during Christmas. They had a history going back years.

And he was, I had to admit, smoking hot.

"You've been dating Eddie?" I asked, trying to make sense of what was happening. "You and Eddie are together, and you didn't tell me?"

"We *were* together. Briefly," Emma said, her face blanching. "We're not now."

"Oh." I blinked. "Oh. Oh, Emma."

"Look, it's fine." Her hand dropped to her stomach. "Eddie was chosen as the alpha of his pack, and I...I couldn't...I don't understand their world. We were supposed to be the alpha pair, and I don't even know what that means. Even though I was human, I had responsibilities, and the other women in the pack were angry, and—" She stopped and took a deep breath. "Yeah, just no."

"It is an oversimplification to say that the alpha male selects his mate. According to our customs, one female eliminates the competition, effectively making herself the only option for the alpha male," Wyatt explained. "Of course, being the alpha, Eddie can make any rules he wants."

"It is common for the alpha pair to be the only pair to mate in a wolf pack. It keeps the pack's numbers under control, as having too many wolves, especially puppies, would be a liability," Lawrence added.

"This is not a hard and fast rule," Wyatt said. "In some packs, the beta pair will be allowed to breed—it all depends on what the alpha pair allows."

The corners of Emma's mouth drew downward, which betrayed the weariness behind her eyes. The light from overhead cast jagged shadows around her frustrated face as the werewolves rambled on.

"True. Regardless, each childless wolf devotes itself entirely to the few puppies born to the alpha pair, ensuring that they grow up to be strong and beneficial members of the pack," Norden finished. "Emma is the alpha female of our pack, our alpha's chosen mate."

"Stop saying that," Emma hissed. "I am *not* a member of your pack." Emma stared at me, the corners of her mouth turning down more deeply. "Astra, tell them that's not how this works."

The three men watched me, their faces as stern and serious as ever.

"I...I don't know," I said. "I'm not a werewolf."

Emma's eyes snapped up to mine, and she shook her head. "Well, neither am I!"

My head was spinning.

I flipped a star card for Damien Elkhart, a snobbish vampire who may or may not have stabbed his friend in a parking lot. A snotty vampire that a vampire retributionist wanted to stick a fork in—a sentiment, frankly, I couldn't disagree with, despite the goddess Athena's demand he live.

Then we had Ivy Masterson, a half-vampire bit against her will, fighting with all her might to cling to the last vestiges of her humanity. What role she had in this still escaped me, but considering two of the three vampires present when she was attacked had become part of this—one dead and another marked for death—I couldn't discount this all had something to do with her.

And swirling around all this was whatever the heck was going on at Sanguine. Vampire religion, Ambrogio belief systems, VampB&B's…it was enough to make my head spin on my neck like Archie's did.

And now Emma, pregnant.

With a werewolf baby.

"I don't understand why you didn't tell me about you and Eddie," I said to Emma as we stood together, alone, on the back porch.

"I was going to," she said.

"When? Before or after the birth?"

She glared at me. "Okay, Ms. *gods don't exist even though I can shoot lightning from my fingers, and this owl is talking to me.* Tell me again how quick you process things. Judge me some more."

"Ouch."

Her face was stony, and her gaze was directed toward the brick buildings that lined the road. "Look, I was just trying to get myself right with it before I had to tell you. It was never a big deal, Astra. It was something I had to work through, and I was doing that." I watched as she sucked in a deep breath and shook her head. "Here's the whole story. I went down to Palm Beach for a couple of weekends. That's all. One thing led to another, and I didn't watch myself. And obviously, I wasn't careful. There. All caught up."

"Are you in love with him?" I asked quietly.

Emma's mouth twisted up slightly. "You have to understand, I've always loved Eddie. When the whole werewolf thing happened, it was crazy. I didn't know what to do—what I was doing." She shrugged. "I wasn't thinking."

We stood quietly in the night breeze.

"There's this hierarchy thing that happens when you get a group of werewolves together. I can't explain it. It's like…a hive mind, I guess. I just don't understand it. That part of him." Emma took a deep breath, and when she let it out, I could see just how upset she was. "What I do know is I can't be a part of it, and it was a mistake to lead him on." She looked at me and held my eyes. "He was so upset when I said I couldn't see him anymore. I thought it was the right thing, but it was...it was like I was bound to him by something greater than either one of us." She patted her stomach. "I guess we know what *that* was now."

"You didn't answer my question."

She glanced at me. "Which one?"

"Whether you're in love with him."

"It's...complicated."

"It's complicated because you're human," I said as something popped into my head. "It's complicated because Eddie is the alpha, and you're a human."

"Thanks, Captain Obvious. Gosh, and you wonder why I never told you," Emma said sarcastically.

I watched her for another moment, then sighed. I didn't want her to be upset. I didn't want her to be mad. And I understood why Emma didn't tell me. Normally blunt and self-assured, Emma had her confidence knocked way down. Anyone would need time to process, and from what I could tell, she was *still* processing.

"I don't understand any of it," she whispered. "I don't understand any of this. And I don't understand how, with everything I know about the paranormal, I let myself get into this situation."

I leaned my head back and looked up at the star-strewn sky. Emma's hand came up and rested on my arm.

"I am sorry," she said. "I'm sorry I didn't tell you. I just wasn't sure what to think about it, much less how to talk about it. And frankly, I had no idea how to talk about it without sounding like a human bigot. Because it's not about Eddie as a person. If Eddie was just Eddie…" she trailed off and then sighed. "It's about the werewolf stuff."

Emma and I stood quietly, watching the night.

"He was pretty mad. Gosh, he was mad," she said.

"Who? Eddie?"

She nodded. "I told him about the baby over the phone."

"You told him on the phone?" I asked, shocked. I stopped there, seeing the stricken look on Emma's face.

"He wanted me to move to Palm Beach so he could take care of me. It didn't matter to him whether we got back together or not, just that I was near. He offered to give me time. He said he wouldn't pressure me. He offered to move here."

"He sounds like a good man."

"I said no. I told him to stay away from me and hung up on him. I'm not even sure why I said it." She exhaled sharply. "Have you ever *felt* like you were doing the right thing, but you *knew* it was the wrong thing at the time? But you did it anyway?"

Every damn day.

"Your head and your heart aren't aligned," I told her.

She swallowed hard and nodded.

"I can't believe I was so stupid," she said, her voice cracking slightly. "So stupid. And now I've made a mess of everything."

I didn't know why Emma thought she'd been stupid. I also didn't know if she was talking about her relationship with Eddie, the pregnancy, or leaving him. All I knew for sure was that my friend was in pain. I sighed and looked up at the night sky. "Chin up, Sullivan. It'll work out. We've all been there."

"Oh, c'mon," she said. "You expect me to believe that you got knocked up by a werewolf in a fancy-schmancy Palm Beach Four Seasons, too?"

The two of us burst out laughing.

* * *

"HOLD UP, HOLD UP, HOLD UP," I said, leaning forward on the couch. "Wouldn't that be considered a descension and not an ascension? If the vampires believe Artemis is going to come *down* from Mount Olympus into a vampire, she would descend. Not ascend."

"I didn't name the thing, Ms. Arden," Wyatt said. He looked around at everyone. "I'm just the messenger. And I don't care what it's called."

Emma, Wyatt, Archie, and I were sitting in the living room while Jason and Aunt Gwennie were in the kitchen, making sandwiches. Lawrence and Norden were patrolling the grounds, not content to rely on "invisible witch fences" to protect Emma.

My mother and Ami were off doing...um, whatever seer things they do in situations like this. They had already placed the knife underneath the couch cushion so I could test our invisibility theory when the vampires came back into the room.

I glanced over at Emma.

Since we'd found out about the baby, my friend looked like she'd aged ten years. I'd hoped all of us knowing would help her, shared burdens and all that. But her eyes were red-rimmed and puffy, and she wore a weary, responsible expression.

And yet, she was Emma.

She worked the case.

"So you're saying," Emma said, "that everyone at that meeting believes that when this ascension —or descension—happens, Artemis will come into this plane of reality and walk the earth in the body of a vampire? Do I have that right?"

Wyatt nodded as Farah sat next to him, staring silently.

"That's a little bit insane," she murmured. "Artemis, a god with god-like superpowers, is going to give all that up to become a bloodsucker?" Emma tilted her head. "That doesn't seem a little bit unlikely to these folks?"

"They're zealots. What they believe doesn't have to make any sense. Those that are not zealots probably know that won't happen," Wyatt said. "My guess is it's a symbol. They're just trying to rally their troops."

"For what?"

Rex flicked his wrist as he entered through the door and tossed a few crumpled pieces of paper into the wastebasket. Damien swaggered behind him, looking bored and disinterested.

"Werewolf?" Rex asked. Wyatt nodded. "Cool. Nice to meet you."

Wyatt dismissed Rex as a threat rather quickly, but his eyes followed Damien like a wolf tracking a bear across the frozen tundra.

"You all are ridiculous, talking about vampires as if you know what's going on," Damien said. "You're taking information from werewolves on vampires?" He flopped into the leather easy chair across from me and kicked his feet up on the coffee table, relaxing. "How does your wolf pack like the idea of Uncle Vampire over here? With a blood tie to both werewolves and vampires, if that kid comes out a witch, too? Damn, it might just be the apocalypse."

"You told *him*?" Emma gasped, staring at Rex furiously.

Rex shook his head. "We could hear you," her brother reminded her.

My brain was furiously sifting through what Damien just said thanks to an itchy tingle on the back of my neck—as if something I just heard related to everything going on. A key. Something important. I felt a sudden sense of foreboding in the pit of my stomach, frustrated because I couldn't pinpoint why I felt this way.

Stupid inexact instincts.

Damien laughed. "Yeah, Rex?" he said. "We heard what? That she's going to have a baby, or that it's probably the Antichrist?" Damien shifted just a tiny bit, and his grin grew. His fangs weren't fully extended, but any smile from a vampire showing pointy teeth always looked deadly.

"Shut up, bloodsucker," Wyatt said, his voice sounding more like a growl.

"Oh, don't look at me," Damien said, kicking his feet back down to the floor and leaning forward. "I'm just joking. Gotta find some way to pass the time."

Rex's head darted from Damien to Wyatt and Farah and then back once again. "Can we kill him now, or do we still have to wait?"

"Just wait," Emma said, her voice firm.

Damien shook his head and chuckled. "You're so cute. It's adorable. Three werewolves, six witches, two vampires, and a witch hunter, all working together. What a crazy thing this is turning out to be, huh?"

"Three werewolves, six witches, one vampire, and a witch hunter, all working together," Emma said, her voice quickly growing cold. "You're not telling us everything you know."

"What am I, chopped liver?" Archie asked,

proving he'd been in Central Florida far too long. "The goddess's own owl! Left off the list!"

Damien was staring intently at Emma. "You would trust a vampire?"

"If that vampire was you?" Emma shook her head and rolled her eyes. "Not for a minute."

Damien smiled again. "You are cute."

"Am *I* cute?" I asked as the conversation devolved. Which, you know, seemed to be the standard modus operandi for any conversation Damien joined.

"In a tough, lesbian way, sure."

Man, I wanted to punch this guy.

Instead, I reached down between the couch cushions and wrapped my hand around the Shroud Blade's handle. "How about now?"

Rex and Damien's jaws simultaneously dropped as I faded from view. Their mouths hung open. Their eyes darted around the living room, searching for some sign of my presence.

"What witchery is this?" Damien whispered, his face pale. "What is that? Is that the Shroud Blade? Is it?"

I stood up so the knife was visible, and I could see their shock register. Damien and Rex were on their feet as I swung the Shroud Blade in a wide arc an arm's length from Damien's face. "No!" He screamed, his hands shooting up to protect himself as he stumbled back, terrified.

"Huh," Emma murmured. "That was unexpected."

I knew what she meant.

Either Damien Elkhart was a good actor (pretending he'd never seen the Shroud Blade before), or Damien Elkhart did not murder his friend Killian Jarrow with it.

It didn't change that I wanted to punch him in the face.

CHAPTER FIFTEEN

We sat around the living room once more, discussing what to do next. We had formulated a plan when Wyatt went outside to check on something in the car. After several minutes he came back into the house, slamming the door behind him.

"Oh, dear lord, what now?" Emma murmured.

Wyatt's face was grim, his eyes were cold, and his hands were fists.

"Lothian Pennington's gone," Wyatt said.

"So what? He's a dog. Maybe he wandered off to chase a car or something," Damien said with an eye roll. "I don't mind having one less dog. Maybe he was going to try to kill me, and your magic scared him away. I don't want a werewolf to attack me. Tonight, I had a witch attempt to stab me. The vampire retri attempted to shoot me. Isn't that the last thing I need? I don't need a dog either. They drool, and their blood tastes bad."

"What are you even talking—" Emma started, but Damien cut her off with a derisive laugh. Emma frowned and glanced at Wyatt, but then she quickly looked back at Damien with suspicion. "You know, the more he talks, the more I wonder if one of us could be the one that's going to try and kill him. Buddy, no one cares about your comfort." She turned back to Wyatt. "Anyway, what do you mean, gone?"

"Vanished. The car in the driveway is there, but he is not." Wyatt didn't look particularly worried, but with werewolves, it was hard to tell.

Emma scratched the back of her head and then sat on a chair and leaned forward, resting her elbows on her knees. "That's strange," she said, her tone serious. "Maybe he accidentally crossed the ward barrier, couldn't get back on the property, and went back to wherever you guys are staying?"

"If that happened, he would patrol outside the barrier. We are pack," Wyatt responded as if that statement answered all of her questions. "There is no reason for Lothian to leave the property. You are on this property. We are here to protect you. That is why we are here. That is all we are here to do."

"Don't you guys have some kind of telepathic communication thing or something?" Jason asked, his face earnest. "Can you call him somehow?"

"We werewolves communicate three ways. Through scent, posture, and vocally. We could track his scent, but to do that, we would have to leave Emma. And considering all that's going on here in Forkbridge—"

"And the posture and scent of this predator," Norden interrupted quietly, shooting a tight glance at Damien.

"Yes, and that," Wyatt agreed, his brow wrinkling. He turned to Jason. "In any case, we can track him through scent, but any attempt to follow his scent will place us in potential danger. We cannot subject Emma and the pup to that."

"Oh, no. Still an autonomous person here. We're not going to do this," Emma warned Wyatt, standing up and stepping in front of the gray-bearded man with determination. "You're not going to treat me like some porcelain doll that needs to be protected from the big bad wolf."

"Okay. Weird analogy," Jason murmured.

"On a few levels," Farah agreed.

"We're trying to keep you safe," Wyatt said, sounding uncertain. His head tilted as he considered Emma's words. "You are a valuable resource to our alpha."

"Dude, I'm a person, not a resource!" Emma shot back hotly, her finger pointed at his chest.

"Oh, my gosh, paranormals are so annoying," I muttered.

"I know, right?" Archie agreed, staring straight at me.

I stuck my tongue out at him.

"Why?" Jason asked.

"Does Lothian have a cell phone?" I asked with some exasperation. "You're all from Palm Beach. You must be wheeler-dealers or businessmen or arms dealers or whatever. Don't you people carry cell phones like everyone else?"

It was a problem with paranormals that lived within the human world.

You had to be more human than paranormal at times. You had to be more paranormal than human at times. When you were in "human" mode, the human solutions to a problem—cell phones, cars, lawyers—were always the first thing that came to mind. It was the supernatural when you were in "paranormal" mode—scenting prey, magic, potions, amulets, psychic visions. Compartmentalizing made life easier in some ways while making it more difficult in others.

In the Ministry, I was almost always on an assignment in the human world, and my first thought tended to be a human solution that wouldn't draw much attention.

Like, you know, calling Lothian and asking him where he was.

On his cell phone.

"I have a cell phone," Damien said.

"Why are you even here again?" I asked out loud.

"You should know, you're the one dragging me all over this stupid—"

"Shut up, Damien," Emma warned, but I could tell she wasn't really angry.

"Yes. Lothian has a cell phone," Wyatt said grudgingly.

"Call it," Emma told him. "Ask him where he is."

Wyatt nodded, pulling out the phone from his pocket and stepping away from the group. Norden and Lawrence, standing beside me, watched him intently.

"Hey, can I ask you guys a question?"

The two werewolves turned to face me at the

same time as if they were linked and had telepathically choreographed their movements. "Yes."

"Why are you all here and Eddie's not? Was he too busy?"

Norden glanced at Emma, who threw up her hands and turned away from us. "Emma has asked Eddie to leave her alone. The alpha is trying to respect his mate's wishes because she is with child, and what she wants is what she should have—"

"Then go back to Palm Beach," Emma snapped irritably.

"—as long as it does not put her in danger," Norden finished with a raised eyebrow. "He wanted to come. In fact, I suspect he is sick with worry. And yet, he is respecting her wishes."

"This is just ridiculous," Emma muttered.

"She is a strong woman," Lawrence murmured.

Norden nodded. "Emma, I cannot challenge your decisions to banish Eddie from your life. But I can say that you will need to respect and honor your mate as a father in order for him to trust your decisions. I imagine it will be difficult for you, as strong and independent as you are, but you must do it. Even if it is difficult. Even if he is driving you crazy with his protective nature. He does so out of love. That I know. Even if you choose to reject his love for you, you have no right to reject his love for your child."

Emma sighed and shook her head, but she didn't argue.

"Are you single?" Farah asked Norden, her eyes dancing.

"Am I what?" he asked distractedly. Seeing Farah's hungry expression once he took his eyes from Emma, Norden wisely chose not to answer.

* * *

"The vampires have him," Wyatt said, holding out the phone toward me. "There is a vampire who says he knows you. He wants to talk to you."

"Who?" I asked, taking the phone.

"I don't know. He won't tell me his name."

"What do you mean, the vampires *have* him?" Jason demanded, standing and stepping toward Wyatt. He tossed his hands up. "What the heck is going on here?"

"Don't worry, Jason," I said, trying to sound as reassuring as I could. "That would be Rudy, I'm sure," I said, pulling the phone from Wyatt's hand. "Hello, Rudy," I said calmly. Emma, Jason, and

Farah crowded around me, straining to hear the conversation.

Damien stood back, smirking.

"How did you know it was me?" Rudy's voice, calm and self-assured, asked me through Wyatt's phone. "Get a sense of a disturbance in the air? One of your sisters do a reading that said your past would come back to haunt you?"

"How did you get Lothian?" I asked instead.

"He's not with me, per se. He's with a friend of mine."

"Why is he with a friend of yours?"

"We had a little chat about knives," Rudy said with a chuckle. "We had a little chat about you."

"He doesn't know anything about me or the Shroud Blade."

"Yes, but I do know he's a member of your best friend's pack now," Rudy responded with a smug chuckle. "What's the old saying? Keep your friends close and your enemies closer? I haven't decided which Lothian is, but I guess that's really going to be up to you, now, won't it?"

"Rudy, quit playing games. What do you want?"

"I already told you, but you decided to ignore me. It didn't work well for you in the Ministry, and it was the wrong choice here,

Astra," he said coolly. "I asked you nicely to return the Shroud Blade. Now, I'm telling you—give me the knife, I give you the werewolf. Everybody's happy."

Return.

He said *return* the Shroud Blade.

"What's the Ascension?" I asked.

"Meet me with the blade, and I'll tell you. Behind Griselda's Ice Cream Shop in half an hour," Rudy said. His voice softened slightly, the previous bravado dialing down just a bit. "Look, Astra, I don't want to hurt the werewolf. I just want the knife. That's all. Don't try anything stupid." He paused. "And come alone."

"I'll see you then," I said, sounding confident and in control.

"She's not going, and she's not bringing the knife," Jason said after I hung up the phone. "There's no way. And if she is going, she's not going alone."

Emma and Damien were standing on either side of me, shoulder to shoulder. Farah, Lawrence, and Wyatt were crowded in front of us. Ami, flipping cards across the room at the kitchen table with Norden, glanced up with a sympathetic expression. In fact, they all looked at Jason as if he was the most naive human on the planet, thinking he could tell me what to do. Even Damien.

"We're not letting her go, right?" Jason said confidently.

Norden and Lawrence looked at each other.

"If Astra wants to go, she'll go," Emma said. "If she wants us to come with her, we will. If she wants us to stay here, we will. Because she knows this guy, Rudy, and we don't. Rex, maybe, can—" Emma turned and looked around, suddenly realizing her brother was no longer in the room. "Wait a minute. Where's Rex?"

"You're not going alone," Jason insisted. "I'm coming with you."

"No," I said. "You're not."

"I'm not going to let you go alone," Jason said, his voice catching. He glanced at Emma, who shook her head at him.

"Astra's never alone. Archie will be there," Emma told my worried boyfriend. "And your girlfriend is perfectly capable of taking care of herself and making her own decisions. As am I." She glared at the three werewolves. "Which is something I wish the men in this room would start to comprehend."

"We all know how capable you are, Emma," said a voice from the front hallway.

Emma tensed with fury.

I wheeled around to see Eddie Renzo, werewolf alpha and father of Emma's baby, standing in the doorway, flanked by Rex and my mother.

Emma crossed her arms and stared at Wyatt accusingly.

"I'm sorry," Wyatt said quietly. "Lothian is missing. I had to tell him."

"You promised," Emma told Eddie, her voice a little shaky, as she moved away from him. "You promised you would stay away."

"*I will never leave a fallen comrade,*" Eddie whispered, reminding her of the line in the Soldier's Creed they both knew well enough from their Army days. "I will not break that or leave it to others." He smiled wistfully. "Not even for you, my dearest love."

Emma looked like she wanted to argue with him, but finally, she nodded her head. I saw her lower lip quiver.

Eddie's last words were said with such conviction and longing that I stepped back, feeling as if I had just crossed the line into a very private, very painful moment.

* * *

WE HAD LITTLE TIME, but it was quickly decided that Eddie and I would travel to Griselda's with Archie for air support, and that I would bring the knife. Jason tried to argue, but Emma convinced him that if the vampires kidnapped him for leverage, he would be more of a liability.

Besides, Emma needed Eddie out of her line of sight. His appearance had knocked her for an emotional loop, and I wanted to give her time.

As I watched the two of them, I knew that Emma had not rejected Eddie because she didn't want him. She appeared to fear how strong her feelings for him were. I could see it all in her face as she watched him: she was terrified of this world he was in, and she feared losing him if she decided to rely on him.

Not that I would know anything about that.

"I suppose you have questions," Eddie said from the passenger seat of my Jeep as we drove toward Griselda's to meet Rudy.

I cast a glance over at him. He was dressed in a brown leather jacket that he said belonged to his father the last time I met him. Even Eddie Renzo's clothing choices reflected the importance he placed on family.

"I probably should, but I don't, really," I said after a brief silence. "Any moron can see how much you love Emma. I think if anyone has questions in this car, it's probably you for me. Though I don't think I have many answers for you," I told him, turning onto Main Street. "I didn't even know the two of you had seen each other until tonight. She didn't tell me."

"I think she was afraid," he said quietly.

"Afraid of what?"

"Of losing me. And of being afraid, really," Eddie said. "She's been through a lot, and she doesn't want to be hurt again. She told me that she couldn't get any more involved in the paranormal than she already was without losing herself. As a human, she couldn't be the mate I needed." He brushed his hand over his dark eyes. "She thinks she's protecting herself by sending me away—but she's really just pushing me away and making sure we're both alone and miserable."

"So, what did you say?"

"I told her—I think it's safe to say that I told her that I couldn't pretend I didn't care about her," he said. "That it would be a lie. That I'm not capable of lying to her. And that if we can't be together, well, we just can't be together. Simple as that. And I told her that we didn't need to talk about it anymore."

I rolled my eyes. "Wow. Men are just...wow."

He frowned at me. "What do you mean?"

"You just told me that she was, more or less, trying to protect herself from getting involved with you. Felt she might fail you somehow," I told him. "Because she knew she couldn't be what you needed, not without changing. Right?"

"Yes, something like that." Eddie's voice was so low I barely heard him.

"And in response," I said, turning to face him and leaning over the console with one eye still on the road, "you said hey, yeah, okay, cool. Love you and all, but since that's your final answer, we don't need to talk about it anymore?"

His face became painfully expressionless.

I couldn't imagine what it was like for him, watching his love for Emma and his dream of a family get stomped by Emma's stubborn refusal to talk through the immense changes that would have to be made and how to deal with them. He was sweet (for a werewolf) and completely in love —but also bullheaded and impossibly idealistic.

"Look, I understand. You were attempting to honor her wishes. It's commendable. And I understand you thought you were doing the right thing. And I'm not suggesting you track her down and force her to talk to you," I told him gently. "But did she say she didn't want to talk about it anymore or did you volunteer that trying to show just how respectful you were?"

"I don't know," Eddie said, looking at me as if he was seeing me for the first time. "I guess she did say something about not talking about it anymore. Or she asked me if there was anything else I had to say, and I...said we didn't have to... talk about it." Eddie appeared to understand as he explained, and his expression became embarrassed.

I laughed. "You're an idiot."

He looked at me sheepishly. "You sound surprised."

"You must understand that she does what she does to protect herself and those she loves. And I understand that you do what you do to keep everyone around you safe," I told him, slowing down as I came to a stop sign. "But you didn't give her a chance to tell you how she really felt, and you didn't give her time to process. Sounds like you just shut the whole thing down."

"That wasn't my intention."

I extended my hand and patted him on the knee. "It's tough when you love someone who can't be what exactly you need them to be. Someone who doesn't know how to accept what you're offering or who needs a little more time to work through it all. But you've got to be brave, and you've got to be honest in order to find a way to make it work. What do you absolutely have to keep doing, though? You have to keep talking."

We pulled into the parking lot behind Griselda's and parked at the far end of the building, out of the way. I slipped the knife into my belt so it wouldn't touch my skin but would still be protected by the vampire repellent bubble I had around me.

Rudy was leaning against his motorcycle, smoking a cigarette. "I thought I said alone," he said as we walked over to meet him.

"Lothian is Eddie's pack member," I told Rudy. "I wasn't going to leave him behind, considering."

The werewolf said nothing. He just stared menacingly.

Rudy's eyes dropped to the knife on my hip. "I wasn't sure you'd bring it."

"I wasn't sure I wouldn't have to use it."

He shook his head and pushed away from the bike. "Well, here's hoping you don't have to. Can I have the blade, then?"

"Can I have the information about the Ascension?"

"And Lothian," Eddie added. "We need Lothian. Unharmed."

I stared Rudy down, but he didn't flinch.

And no one spoke.

"Okay, is he truly alone?" I inquired of Eddie. "Or are we surrounded by vampires waiting to strike at the edge of the parking lot?" The wolf twitched his nose. "Because I can't believe he thinks I'm just going to hand this to him so he can immediately leave us here without the information or Lothian."

"He's alone," Eddie told me, not taking his eyes off the vampire.

"Knife first," Rudy said and held out his hand. "It's important."

It was a standoff, and I hated a standoff.

"Rudy," I said. "I can give you the knife, but I'm not going to risk Lothian. If you lay a hand on him, Eddie here just might kill you."

It was the wrong thing to say.

Rudy's eyes flashed, and he took a menacing step toward me. "Don't you threaten me! You have no idea what's going on, and you and your friends have done nothing but get in my way since I got here," he told me, his voice cold and low. "I came here to meet you alone. Give me the benefit of the doubt for once. Give me the knife. I'll tell you what you want to know." He stared at my hip. "But not until I have that weapon."

I stared back for a long moment, weighing the consequences of what I was about to do. Decided that I didn't have much of a choice.

"Fine," I told him as I handed him the knife, which he grabbed with a gloved hand. "But you're on a short leash because I don't know why you need the knife, and I don't know what you're going to do with it."

Rudy tapped his cell phone and told whoever was at the other end to let the captured werewolf go.

"Thank you," Eddie said simply.

"Now, what is the Ascension?" I asked after he tapped his phone to hang up.

Rudy glanced at Eddie. Then he nodded. "It's a fraud."

CHAPTER SIXTEEN

"It's a prophecy," Rudy said, sucking on his cigarette. "That's the first thing you need to know. Like every other prophecy, it's made of rumors, stories run amok and embellished over decades."

I raised my eyebrow. "Oh?"

"Yep. Someone, at some point in history, said something was going to happen, and that idea spread like wildfire with every generation after, until the Ascension became this great legend, this monumental building block of fate determined to bring about some new era. It's all bull, though. Vampires have just been conned into believing them."

"So you don't believe in prophecy," Eddie Renzo said to Rudy.

"I didn't say that," Rudy answered. "I don't know what I believe. Maybe there's prophecy magic. But I know what I don't believe. I don't believe in heaven. Or hell. Or God. Or gods and goddesses. At least not ones that answer any of our prayers." He threw his cigarette down on the asphalt and ground it beneath his boot. "I was a witch. Now I'm a vampire. And the only thing I've seen in either life with my own eyes are manipulative people with delusions of grandeur chasing power."

Eddie leaned over, picked up the cigarette butt, and pocketed it.

"Okay. Cynical, but I get it. You're a member of the Ambrogio, though, so I'm not sure how what you just said squares with what you do," I pointed out.

"Because that's where the power is. I play the game." He shrugged. "I don't know if the Ambrogio is any different from any other bunch of people looking for a way to justify their power. But I suspect not. Gods," Rudy scoffed, "are just made up stories to control people."

Eddie and I looked at one another.

"What?" Rudy asked.

"Astra and I spent Christmas with a few of the Greek gods," Eddie told him, his voice dry. "They're more than stories."

"I don't care what you think you saw." Rudy tapped the side of his head. "It was all in here. You see what you expect to see."

"You have no idea what I saw, vamp," Eddie snapped.

"If you two believe in fairy tales, there's no point in telling you anything more, really," Rudy said, his lips pulled back and his fangs showing. "If you believe in that garbage, you two are a couple of Ambrogio pawns. That's all you'll ever be. Gods aren't real. You're an idiot if you think they are." He turned his back to me and started to get on his bike without looking back.

Out of the corner of my eye, I saw Eddie close his hands into fists, and my stomach churned in anticipation of a fight erupting. So when Rudy put his foot on his bike kickstand, I tried to move between them.

I wasn't fast enough.

Rudy never saw the fist coming.

"Okay, enough, enough, enough!" I said, pushing against Eddie to back him away from Rudy—who, shockingly, just jumped off the bike to stand on his feet instead of going for Eddie's throat. "You didn't need to do that, Eddie—and Rudy, you made an agreement to tell us about this stupid Ascension! You didn't predicate it on our religious beliefs—or lack thereof!"

"That was for Lothian," Eddie told Rudy ominously.

"Next time, doggy, I'll tear you apart." Rudy shook his finger at Eddie like he was the biker vampire sword of Damocles. "You get one pass. One."

Eddie stepped back from Rudy and me, and I breathed a sigh of relief.

"Okay, let's drop the god talk, back up, and see if we can fill some of these blank spots in," I breathed, extending my hand toward Rudy. "Who's Lila Redmond? The Ambrogio administrator—you both have the same last name. Why is that?"

Rudy tensed. "She's my wife." His hands went up to cover his mouth after a brief hesitation that had me wondering what he would do. Then he shrugged and dropped them. "She's my wife. It's partly why I'm with the Ambrogio." His face fell. "And why I'm a vampire."

* * *

THE STORY he told next was shocking—and yet not surprising.

Lila hid a vampire Rudy had been pursuing, a typical Ministry catch and secure mission. Lila admired his intelligence and tenacity as he pursued her, and he was astounded by how she always seemed one step ahead. He gradually grew to admire her.

Lila and Rudy circled each other like a cat and a mouse as they crisscrossed Egypt. Rudy mistook himself for the cat, but it was the other way around.

"Vampires can love," he admitted, shifting uncomfortably on the asphalt under the parking lot light. "And by that time, I loved her. She was amazing—mysterious and tough and beautiful and...when she made the offer, I took it."

"When she made the *offer*," I repeated.

"Yes."

"And the soldiers that came to rescue you?" I asked through clenched teeth. "What about them? Did you have to kill them? Was there nothing of your humanity left in you? No remorse that you took their lives?"

"First, I didn't."

"That makes it better somehow?"

"Lila knew the Ministry would never stop

hunting me if they knew it was my choice to turn," Rudy admitted. "She thought if you all thought I was turned by force, you'd likely leave me alone. Eventually."

"Why would that matter?" I asked, my forehead crinkling with confusion. A migraine headache loomed, threatening to strike me like a lightning bolt at any moment. "Whether you chose to, whether you were forced...it's all the same. You're still a vampire."

"A vampire that fights the transition is much stronger at the end of it," Rudy explained. "I'm surprised you weren't aware of it. Though I didn't realize that until I was turned, so that makes sense." He nodded to himself. "The Ministry is well aware of that vampire lore, though. They knew even if they never bothered to tell us."

The information hit me like a physical blow. "So to make it look like you were too tough to be caught, you killed my entire—"

"Again—I did not," he insisted, cutting me off. "Lila did. My wife can be quite ruthless when she wants to be," he said proudly, ironically describing every vampire that ever lived. "I understood why she did it. You all were coming after me, and she was protecting me. Not that it's an excuse."

"You could have stopped her," I said.

"I could not have."

I felt the rage building and came close to punching him in the face myself, but with a deep, cleansing breath, I decided to let it go. We were at an unnecessary impasse. I could try to tell him how I felt, but he was so caught up in his new vampire life he would not have heard a word I said. What are a few dead former soldiers?

"What's the Ascension?" I asked once more, teeth still clenched.

"The vampire goddess made manifest on earth. You know, a fraud," he said. He reminded me of a sociopath who argues over inconsequential things to cover up his creepy absence of feeling about the things he should be sorry for. "The Ambrogio created her to make the Ascension seem real."

"Wait, wait—her. Who's *her*?"

"Some daughter of one of the Ambrogio vampires," Rudy said, shrugging. "But something went wrong, and they can't get to her. She was supposed to be totally controllable, able to pretend she was Artemis incarnate or something."

I frowned. "Controllable how? Why?"

"You really don't know much about vampires, do you?" Rudy asked insultingly. "The girl was a human daughter of a high-up Ambrogio vampire. Once she was turned, they would have a human blood tie. He turned her, which would give her a double blood tie to him—meaning Daddy can control his dear daughter like she was a puppet on a string."

"But he didn't bite her," I whispered. "He refused to."

"That can't be true." Rudy looked at me, surprised. "How do you know that?"

"Because I think I know the vampire," I told him. "And the daughter."

Rudy suddenly looked tense and agitated. "Who? Who is it?"

"You don't know?"

"Would I be asking you if I did?" he said, the corners of his mouth turning down. "You know I can't read you in the same way I can others. The dog doesn't know—I've already sifted through his mind. So, tell me. Who is she?"

"Why do you need to know?" Eddie asked him.

Rudy looked frustrated.

The werewolf looked at me. "I don't trust him."

"Well, you'd better," the vampire responded, taking another step toward me. "My wife's life may depend on finding out who that vampire is. She is the admin. I know you don't know what that means, but it's important. She's important. And if the Ascension takes place—or if people think the Ascension takes place—*she's* displaced from her position. And if that happens?" Rudy paced so fast my eye could barely mark his movements. "Astra, please. You have to tell me. I have to stop this."

"Why? Just tell me why."

"Thousands of vampires die during the Ascension, and those chosen ones that travel the world wiping out non-Ambrogio vampires (or just those not adequately adhering to the myth) spend the rest of the year absorbing the power of the vampires they've killed," Rudy said through clenched teeth. "This thing will start a vampire civil war the likes of which history has never seen before, and the ascended vampires are more powerful than ever." His eyes narrowed. "And much harder to kill."

"But the daughter you talked about?" I said. "She hasn't turned. If she is who I think she is— and I feel like she has to be—you can't get at her. None of you can. She's in a town with wards that protect everyone within it from vampires."

"I told you," Rudy said with frustration. "It's all

fake. It would have helped for it to be her, but it doesn't have to be her. It's a fraud. People just have to *believe* it's real."

* * *

A CHILD AT THE CENTER.

Ivy Masterson.

It had to be.

Which means Killian Jar—um, Masterson was killed…*six months* after she was turned? But why? Why did so much time pass after his daughter was turned by…I frowned. But she was turned by Damien. So, that made little sense.

Did Rudy kill him? To stop this Ascension thing?

It seemed logical—except he didn't seem to know who Ivy was, so he couldn't know who Killian was.

First, I needed to make sure I was right.

"Stay here, both of you—and don't attack each other, please," I said and walked a few feet away, even though it was pointless. If both of those guys wanted to hear what I had to say on this phone call, they were more than capable.

"Hello?"

"Ayla? It's Astra. I need you to ask—"

"Aunt Gertie's was already way ahead of you," Ayla answered, sounding inexplicably upbeat. "I asked Killian, and he says yes. He's Ivy's father. His human name was Kevin Masterson, and he used to be married to Taylor Masterson. They divorced when Ivy was really young," she went on, "and then he met Adriana Kingsley. Once she turned him, he didn't want to put Ivy or Taylor at risk, so he let them think he was dead. Which, I mean, he was. Sort of."

"But Ivy met him—did she not recognize him?"

Ayla laughed. "There aren't exactly pictures of him up, Astra. If my father walked in and said hello, I'd have no idea who he was, either. It was like that. And he didn't tell her on Halloween. He was supposed to turn her, but at the last minute, he refused to let her be made a pawn."

I frowned. "Do they know? That Killian is her father?"

"I told them both a few minutes ago. Mrs. Masterson is demanding that Althea resurrect Killian—Kevin—so she can kill him again for putting their daughter through so much pain. Althea is trying to explain that she doesn't know how, but she's now off spinning in different directions of how a potion might work."

"Does Althea know how to un-vamp the kid yet?"

"Yeah, so that's a real conundrum. Althea said she could do it, but she has to have Damien here to do it because he was the one that bit her. Basically, she can cut both of them and give Ivy a potion—actually, I think she does the potion first —anyway, Damien's vamp blood will ooze on out of her and ooze back into him. Poof, no more Ivy vampire."

I knew there had to be a reason the goddess wanted Damien alive.

And there it was.

Right there.

I covered my eyes with my hands. "But Damien can't go into Cassandra. The town has wards against vampires." I glanced back at Rudy. With what he just said, there's no way I could bring Ivy out from behind that shield. Even though Killian was dead, they were still planning on using her if they could—and if the vampire Purge was about to begin, a half-vamp who refused to turn might be at the top of the kill list. "We can't bring him in, and we can't bring her out."

"Yeah, Astra, I know. That's why I said it was a conundrum," Ayla responded.

I looked back at Rudy.

Ivy was at risk from whatever this Ascension was. If I could help Rudy stop that, I'd be able to help Ivy without having to worry about the entire Ambrogio vampire population pursuing me to further victimize Ivy.

The vampire at the center of the Ascension fraud was most likely the vampire who murdered Killian/Kevin. They switched to Plan B after failing to get Ivy out from behind Cassandra's wards—and wanted to make sure Plan A didn't come back to bite them in the rear.

"Okay, just stay there," I said to Ayla. "I'll call you back."

* * *

"Is that your blade?" I asked Rudy, pointing to his hip.

"You mean did I take it with me as a souvenir of my time in the military?" he asked, his hand drifting down to the pommel. "I did, and it is."

"How'd you lose control of it?" I asked, not accusing him outright of murder—but, well, the implication led my mind, resting on the surface and available to be plucked by any half-decent psychic vamp with half a brain.

"It vanished from my belongings at the Ambrogio house in Atlanta where I was staying," he said, his expression unreadable. "At the house, I met Damien—and there were two other vampires in the room with us at the time. The blade was gone when they left." He said that so calmly, so matter-of-factly. He didn't seem to care one bit about losing it.

Vampires were weird.

"Do you remember their names, at least?"

"Well, of course, I know that—Lila, my wife, was one."

"And the other?"

"Adriana Kingsley."

"Vampires!" Archie hooted from the branches above the parking lot. "Down Main Street, on foot! Headed your way!"

Rudy looked up. "What was that?"

"Trouble," Eddie Renzo muttered as he turned toward the road.

CHAPTER SEVENTEEN

The vampires were coming.

I could feel it in the air, a thickening of the tension that made the hair on my arms stand up. I suddenly felt an unexplainable desire for rain, a real downpour with thunder and lightning and wind whipping the palm trees. With vampires on the way, it was a silly thought to have, but I had always enjoyed a good storm.

Eddie reached for his gun, preparing for a fight.

"Don't," I told him. "We don't know why they're coming."

"How many?" Eddie asked, looking up.

"I can't tell," Archie said from his perch in the

tree. "They're spread out. At least a dozen that I can see."

"That's not good," Rudy muttered.

"Okay, maybe you should pull out the gun," I told Eddie.

Rudy turned to me. "You need to get out of here, Astra. If there's a dozen of them headed this way, they mean business."

I still wasn't sure whether Rudy was friend or foe, so I couldn't help but be on alert around him. As a human, Rudy could always be trusted…well, mostly. His recklessness could cause problems, but I always believed in his integrity.

At least I did until two of my soldiers wound up dead at his wife's hands.

In any case, his advice was ridiculous—vamps could easily catch me.

"And how am I supposed to do that, genius?" I asked with an eye roll. "You're all faster than me, so your suggestion is pointless, anyway." I glanced at Eddie. The werewolf was the one in real danger here. The vampires making their way across our small town couldn't attack me, but they could attack him. "You need to go. Shift, and go. I'll stay and find out what they want."

"I don't think so," Eddie said firmly. "I'm not leaving you here with a bunch of vampires."

"And I'm not keeping you here to potentially get slaughtered. Even if *I* made it through this interaction unscathed, Emma would absolutely end me if I went back to Arden House to tell her that her baby daddy became vamp food," I shot back. "So we're at a bit of an impasse. And by impasse, I mean we're not discussing this anymore, and you're going to do what I'm telling you." At the mention of Emma, Eddie's face grew concerned. "Dude, I swear—I have defenses. I'll be fine. They can't hurt me."

Rudy sighed. "Astra's right. We don't have time for this. Eddie, shift and go. I'll stay with Astra."

"Is that supposed to make me feel better?" Eddie asked Rudy. "Because I have to tell you—it doesn't make me feel better."

Before I could urge him on one more time, Eddie shifted into his wolf form. He came up to me, his large wolf head even with my waist, and nuzzled my hand with his nose. "I'll be okay," I whispered. "You have to go, Eddie."

Eddie pulled back, sniffed the air, and turned his head up to look at me. His eyes were large and black, framed by long tufts of hair that hung down around his face. His thick tail swept back and forth behind him as he stood there, looking at me with an intensity I couldn't understand.

With a grunt, he took off running, disappearing into the woods.

* * *

WE WAITED for what seemed like hours, but it was probably only minutes.

I grew more and more anxious with each passing second. Yes, Althea's potion provided me with an excellent defense against the thirteen or so vampires I was about to confront in a parking lot—but I was still about to confront at least *thirteen vampires*, none of whom I trusted.

Rudy murmured reassurance, but I didn't trust him—especially since he seemed as on edge as I was and especially since he'd previously told me to run.

Finally, we saw them.

Vampires, creeping around the building like spiders—they moved slowly, with predatory energy. Lila, Rudy's wife, was with them, looking smug as ever. And Adriana Kingsley was there too, her face a mask of cold anger. "Where is Damien?" Adriana asked. "Why have you kidnapped one of our kind, witch?"

Oh, I don't think so.

Rudy and I exchanged a look.

I stepped forward, glaring at her. "Damien Elkhart has not been kidnapped. He figures that if he comes out from behind my family's wards, he'll be the next one to die," I pointed out. "Not paranoia considering his friend Killian was stabbed with that knife." I pointed toward Rudy's hip. "Why wouldn't he be next?"

"Damien would never hide from me," she said angrily. "You have taken him hostage for some reason. Or you gave him to the vampire retributionist."

"Asked and answered, Ms. Kingsley," I replied.

"You think knowing my name gives you some kind of upper hand here? Is that supposed to intimidate me?" Adriana stepped toward me, her eyes narrowing. "You have no idea what you're dealing with," she said.

"I know exactly *who* I'm dealing with," I told her, my voice dripping with venom. "A murderer. You killed Killian."

Rudy stepped forward, putting himself between Adriana and me. "Let's not start this by tossing around unfounded accusations at each other," he said calmly. "Astra just wants to talk. I'm sure that's true for you all, as well."

Adriana's eyes flicked to Rudy, and she sneered. "Who's side are you on? We have nothing to talk about." Adriana looked at Lila. "Your husband has betrayed us! That Shroud Blade knife isn't hanging from *my* waist," she said. "It's hanging from the ex-witch's waist. And he knew this Astra witch! The two of them probably killed Killian Jarrow, and now they're trying to deflect blame onto me." She stared back at Rudy and me. "It won't work."

Rudy stepped forward, his hand outstretched in a placating gesture. "My wife knows me well enough to be sure your accusations are meaningless, so you may as well stop. Don't confuse the issue even more than it is, Adriana. Astra is not accusing you—"

"Oh, no, I am," I told him. "I absolutely am."

Before Rudy could say anything else, I took several steps forward, getting right in Adriana's face. "You *killed* Killian," I said again, my voice loud and clear, my pointed (now un-gloved) finger inches from her. "You did it. You know it. I know it. And I'm going to make sure you pay for it."

So, confession time. I wasn't sure.

But I *was* close enough to poke my finger at her exposed skin just above the plunging neckline as I spoke. In the brief moments of contact, the image of the knife plunging into Killian's chest flashed within my mind, a first-person view of his fear face to face. A vantage point that could only be seen by the invisible killer.

She gasped as she saw what I saw.

I winked. "Didn't know I could do that, didja?"

Adriana's face was a mask of cold anger, but she said nothing. Her eyes cast about as if she was trying to figure out how much the others had seen and how much spinning she would have to do to explain the image away.

If Adriana was speechless, the other vampires were becoming restless, muttering to one another and shifting from foot to foot as they each picked up on the psychic image I had allowed to float in the forefront of my mind.

Okay, maybe I broadcasted it.

Loudly.

"Maybe the witch is using magic," one whispered to another.

"It is the witch's own memory, surely," the other whispered back, her voice unsure. "The hand was invisible. So how do we know?"

"Yeah, so, the thing is? Astra was in the club when Killian was murdered," a third said, his voice warily uncertain. "She couldn't have killed him. I saw her at the bar. Even witches can't be in two places at once." He glanced at me. "Damien was locked in a room with her and the retributionist, too. He didn't kill them, and he must know more than we do."

"The investigator has been with the witch," another called out, louder now. "Are you telling me an Ambrogio investigator—one that has spoken to her over and over—never picked up on the fact that she was the murderer?"

I took a step back, glancing at Rudy. He looked as surprised as a vampire was capable of looking. "I did not," he said. "Nothing Astra has said or done made me suspicious that she could have killed Killian. Not really. She had no reason to." He looked at Adriana. "But you did."

"Oh, stop it," Adriana snapped. "Now you all know—Astra Arden killed Killian Jarrow. It lives in her little pea-brained mind. We should just kill the witch and be done with it."

"The witch that just vowed revenge on you for a vampire death?" Lila asked her quietly. "I think not, Adriana."

* * *

RUDY'S WIFE STEPPED FORWARD, her eyes narrowed. "Astra, was the memory yours or Adriana's?" she asked.

"Hers."

"Liar!" Adriana shouted.

"Okay, to be honest—I wasn't completely positive she killed Killian until I touched her, but I was darn close to it," I replied. "It's the only thing that makes sense. She was there the night that Killian refused to turn his daughter; she was angry at him for not doing what she demanded—and that got me to thinking. *Why* would she demand that Killian turn his daughter into a vampire if she wasn't the person setting up this Ascension thing?" A murmur went through the crowd of vampires, and Adriana took a step back, her face pale. "Maybe she got Damien to bite Ivy hoping that between the two of them, she could still control her. I don't know. But eventually, I realized she's the one pushing this Ascension vampire apocalypse theater. She has to be."

Lila considered this for a moment, then turned to Adriana. "Is this true?" she asked. "Have you been trying to manufacture a divine visit in order to displace the Ambrogio leadership and me? Or worse—to slaughter your fellow vampires with impunity?"

"No, it's not true! Are you going to listen to this witch instead of me, a vampire sister? She has no proof because she is a liar," Adriana said, but her voice was shaking ever so slightly. "Lila, you know I am loyal to you! I would never kill another vampire!"

"Yeah, you would. And you did," I said.

"It makes sense, my love," Rudy said to Lila, his expression sad.

"You're going to believe a witch over me? And an ex-witch that probably has no loyalty to us at all?" Adriana shouted. "What proof is there of anything this woman is saying?"

"I don't have proof, but once you left Rudy in Atlanta, his knife was missing. Damien knew the name of it, and he's *your* buddy." I tilted my head. "I think you decided to get rid of anyone that witnessed your preparation as this thing got closer, and you couldn't get to Ivy." I glanced at Lila. "Maybe so the Ambrogio didn't know how much you faked in order to get religious permission to whack a bunch of vampires."

"You don't know what you're talking about," Adriana hissed, but her voice betrayed a nervous unsteadiness she could not fully mask.

Lila turned back to me, her eyebrows raised in

surprise. "Astra, how do you know all this? Who is Ivy?" she asked.

"My sister is with the half-vampire Adriana demanded be turned against her will," I responded, my fury leaking through my words. "We're trying to help her regain her humanity." I looked at Adriana. "The girl's name is Ivy Masterson. She's the human daughter of Killian Jarrow, and Adriana demanded he turn her. He refused."

I closed my eyes and played the scene from the basement as clearly as I could remember it, hoping the vampires were as offended by it as I was. A low growl came from the gathered group's direction, and when I opened my eyes, I watched Adriana take another step back, her face now ghostly white.

"It's not true! This is all a lie! She's a witch, and she's using magic to fool you all!" she cried, but her voice was trembling, and her eyes darted around the parking lot, looking for an escape route.

"Stop her," Lila ordered calmly, and several vampires obeyed immediately, their expressions hardening as they realized what was happening.

The vampires were upon her in an instant, their fingers digging into her flesh as they immobilized her. She fought against them, kicking and screaming, but it was no use. They were too strong.

Lila stepped forward, her face a mask of cold fury. "Adriana," she said in a dangerous voice. "You are accused of killing Killian Jarrow, a vampire that once shared your own nest. A vampire you turned. It is the most grievous of betrayals. What do you have to say for yourself?"

Adriana's eyes widened in terror, and she shook her head frantically. "No, no, you don't understand! I was doing it for us! For the Ambrogio! So we could be stronger!"

"What arrogance," Lila whispered. "To think that a vampire that would *force another to join our kind* believed she knew what was best for all of us." The Ambrogio admin bowed her head. "You have embarrassed us. You're an embarrassment."

Okay, I probably would have picked a stronger word there.

But...yeah.

Vampires are weird.

Adriana hesitated for a moment before she spoke. "I would do it again," she said, her voice shaking. "Killian was going to tell you what I'd done. He was going to ruin everything. I couldn't let him do that. I had to stop him."

"You're the worst kind of vampire," Lila said, her eyes narrowing. "You killed him so he would never tell anyone what you did because you could not face the truth of your own actions? Then you are a coward as well as a killer. The Ambrogio deserve better than that."

Adriana looked away from Lila, struggling to keep the tears in check. "As I said—I did what I had to do, and I would do it again if necessary. Killian was going to tell you what I'd done and ruin everything for me."

"And yet, here we are," I said cheerfully, holding my hands up. "All ruined."

Archie flew down from the trees and landed on Adriana's head. With a wag of his tail feather, the owl pooped on her hair as the shocked vampires looked on. "Now everything's ruined," he told her smugly. The vampires stared at Adriana in disgust, and she looked as if she might be sick.

"Get her out of here," Lila ordered with confident authority, and the vampires all obeyed in unison, dragging Adriana out of the parking lot and back the way they came.

Archie flew to my shoulder.

"Don't even think about it," I warned him.

"I would never," he scoffed. Then the owl

paused and tilted his head. "Well, maybe not never, but it's highly unlikely."

As the vampires disappeared with Adriana into the night, I turned to Rudy and Lila. "I take it you're going to handle her? About murdering Killian, I mean."

Lila sighed and nodded her head. "And trying to overthrow the elites, yes," she assured me. "I'd also like to get my hands on Damien Elkhart, Ms. Arden. It seems clear to me he had a role in this insurrection as well."

"No, I don't think so. I need him for something." I shook my head.

"What could you possibly need him for?" Lila asked, her brow furrowed in confusion.

I turned to her and Rudy. "He's the key to turning Ivy Masterson back into a human being." I paused. "Or stopping her from turning into a vampire. I'm not really clear on the specifics, but I know I need him to help her."

Rudy's eyes widened. "You can stop a vampire from turning?"

"I can't, but my sister's figured out how to do it," I replied. "And once I do that, I've promised the vampire retributionist that she can…um, serve Damien some retribution for turning Ivy without her consent."

Lila was still frowning, but after glancing at Rudy—who nodded ever so slightly—she nodded slowly. "Very well, Ms. Arden. We will leave Damien to you. Please contact us through Rex if you should need our assistance."

"Considering you killed two of my men back in the day to get a boyfriend, Lila, I can almost promise you I won't be doing that," I told her. "I don't trust you."

Rudy and Lila both looked uncomfortable with my comment. Lila cleared her throat before speaking up. "I'm sorry for what happened with your soldiers," she said, sounding a bit guilty. "It was a long time ago, and we were both young and foolish."

It wasn't even ten years ago. In the grand scheme of things, these immortals were probably still children.

"We were," Rudy agreed. "But we're not anymore. We're different people now, Astra, and we would not do what we did again."

"I don't care," I told them coldly. "Once was enough."

Lila stared at me for a minute before she nodded reluctantly, then turned around and walked away. Rudy immediately followed behind her without saying anything further. One thing about vampires. When they decided nothing more could be done, they walked away without so much as a look back.

"You know, I know what it's like to want revenge, and I know how satisfying it can be. But trust me, it's not worth it in the end," Archie said quietly.

I watched the vampires disappear into the night and wondered whether Archie was right.

CHAPTER EIGHTEEN

I met back up with Emma and Eddie on the edge of Cassandra's border, a thin parkland forest that formed a buffer between Cassandra's warded territory and that area vampires could roam freely. We walked together toward Ivy's house—Rex, Farah, and Damien waited on the edge of the wards in a small clearing.

The whole way there, I filled them in on what had happened.

Emma fumed and grumbled passive-aggressively the whole way.

"First and foremost, I'm irritated that you stayed there alone and sent Eddie home. Second, I can't believe you agreed to let those vampires take Adriana rather than dealing with her yourself!" Emma exclaimed when I finished telling my story. "Rudy kidnapped Lothian just to lure us into talking to him! These people can't be trusted. What if they let her go, and she comes back here for revenge or something?"

"What did you want me to do, stake her? I'm not the paranormal sheriff of Central Florida. Look, I get the paranoia, but they won't," I told her confidently. "They've got their own problems to deal with. They're not going to come back to Forkbridge anytime soon. They have nothing to deal with here. Not anymore."

"What about Rex's club?"

"How would I know? Ask Rex."

Emma argued over every move I made without her, her faith in her paranormal expertise growing because of the furry bun she had in the oven—but I smiled at every criticism. Eventually, she ran out of issues with my behavior and finally allowed herself to look relieved that vampire Armageddon had been avoided.

Well. Almost.

One person's personal Armageddon still needed to be dealt with.

As we walked across the lawn, I could see Ivy

standing in the window, silhouetted by a lamp behind her, her slender arms pressed against the glass. She looked worried but not miserable or like she was in pain, so that was a good sign. Hopefully, this would all be over soon, and then she could go back to her normal life.

I knocked louder than I had intended, and Althea's petite frame appeared in the doorway a moment later. Her eyes were wide, and she quickly beckoned us in, a surprised expression quickly melting away as she directed us into the house. "Sorry. I was brain-deep in the final prep for this shindig, and I forgot you were on your way."

"I just talked to you on the phone twenty minutes ago," I pointed out.

"I get focused, that's all," she said and hurried toward a table.

Ivy stood to the side, her shoulder pressed against the wall. Her eyes flickered around the room restlessly, jumping from one face to another. She hadn't spoken a word since we had arrived, and she stood so rigidly that I was afraid to speak in case I startled her. She looked like the walking dead, with skin so pale it was translucent. Dark circles formed beneath her eyes. "Hi, Astra," she whispered.

"What happened?" I asked her, my eyes narrowing. "You look terrible again."

"Wow, aren't you Suzy Sunshine, big sister," Ayla said with a tone of voice that dripped with sarcasm. "The Ministry just skipped right over etiquette classes, huh? No cotillions for the soldiers?"

"It was the military, not a finishing school," I said with a roll of my eyes.

"Aunt Gertie says that's no excuse," my youngest sister popped back.

"I'm just nervous, that's all," Ivy responded, her voice low and shaky. "This is my last hope, really. My only hope now."

Ayla nodded, turned toward Emma, and smiled excitedly. With a clear intent of changing the subject and the tone in the room, she rushed over and congratulated her on being pregnant. "That's amazing news! When are you due?"

"We don't know yet," Emma replied, looking slightly embarrassed. "It's still early days." She looked up at Eddie. "I need to have a discussion with Eddie about carrying a werewolf baby. I don't even know if I can go to a regular doctor or if there are doctors for this, or—"

"We can work it all out," he assured her.

"Heck, my mom's one of the best healers in

the entire world. And Aunt Gwennie's an awesome midwife. I mean, Mom is, too, and everything, but I don't know that she'd be the supportive, comforting one. Like, *I* would pick Aunt Gwennie over Mom. Well, anyway, congratulations," Ayla said again, giving them both a hug. "I'm so happy for you!"

I noticed Emma's use of *we* instead of *I*, and Eddie's response using the same. Their tones and energies were slightly different, too—her voice sounded calmer. His expression seemed more settled.

I also saw Ivy's red-rimmed eyes well up with tears.

"That will be you one day, too," I told her sincerely without thinking. I paused for a moment before adding, "Not that you'll be dating a werewolf as a human, I mean."

"Not that there's anything wrong with that," Althea called from the table where she was preparing the potions for Ivy's un-vampiring.

"You're right," Ivy told me as she sat down on the couch next to her mother. "Helping me isn't your responsibility, I know. And the guru says that you all are the most talented witches there are. I should have faith," she added with a sigh as she crossed her legs delicately. It was obvious that she had been crying earlier; traces of black mascara—I think—faintly stained her cheeks. "I don't doubt your abilities. I just…"

"You're ready to get your life back," Ayla shrugged. "We get it."

"And if we can help, it's our responsibility to help," I told her.

"Okay, I'm ready." Althea picked up her pack and slung it across her back. The glass bottles within made a jingling sound.

"Okay, then. We should probably head out now," I said as I moved toward the door.

"Mom, I don't want you to come with us," Ivy told her mother as she stood up.

"What? Why not?" Taylor Masterson asked, her eyes wide with surprise.

"I'm sure this will work. But I don't know how it will work, and if something goes wrong, I…I don't want you there to see it. You've had to see more than you should have because of my stupid choices—"

"Your father—"

"No, Mom," Ivy said firmly. "You need to stay here. Please."

Taylor Masterson looked like she would argue, but then she nodded and sat back down. "Okay. Be careful." She glared fiercely at a spot in the room I assumed contained the ghost of Killian Jarrow, a.k.a. Kevin Masterson. "If something happens to her, Kevin, I *will* find a way to haunt *you*."

We filed out of the room, Ayla leading the way into the darkness.

* * *

WE ARRIVED at the front of the clearing, the wards that kept the vampires out of Cassandra conveniently cutting straight through the center. The air was thick with the scent of pine and wood smoke, and in the center of the clearing was a small fire, over which a tripod supported a black cauldron. A picnic table was set up beside the fire, and Althea quickly arranged a collection of bottles and jars on it.

"What is this about?" Damien asked, looking concerned.

Oh, right.

We never bothered to tell him what was going on.

"Don't worry about it," Farah said. "You're going to do something good for once in your miserable life." She snorted. "It might be the last thing you do, so you're welcome."

Damien took that as an insult. "What the hell is that supposed to mean?"

"You're going to help Ivy un-vampire herself, Damien," Ayla said as she arranged bottles on the table. "You never should have turned her against her will, and we're all here to help you undo that mistake."

"What? How am I supposed to do that?" Damien asked, looking more confused than ever. No one answered, but as Damien absorbed this information, his expression changed from one of confusion to one of dawning realization—and then horror. "No," he said, stepping back from the table. "I can't do that. You're not doing magic on me. It could kill me!"

"You're already dead, moron," Archie called from a branch above.

"You *can* do that—safely—with our help. You'll see," Althea said as she finished her preparations and turned to face us. "Ivy, you need to drink this." She held out a small glass bottle filled with a murky green liquid.

Ivy took the bottle and unscrewed the cap. She looked at Althea for a moment before downing the contents in one go. She made a face as she handed the empty bottle back. "That was disgusting! What was it?"

"Just some herbs that will help your body adjust to being human again," she explained. "I'm hoping that will take the edge off the transition. It wasn't necessary, but I want to make this as painless as I can for you."

"What about me?" Damien asked, looking faintly nervous.

"We just need you to slice a vein, dude," Althea said matter-of-factly as she finished her preparations and stepped back from the table. "As your blood and venom in her body make its way home where it belongs, the healing process I just kick-started with that drink will reverse the effects of the vampire venom on Ivy and allow her body to start producing its own healthy blood again—without your unwelcome contribution."

Ivy nodded and asked. "So, what do I do now?"

Althea laid the two down on the ground next to one another, Ivy safely within the boundaries of Cassandra and Damien Elkhart just outside of the boundary.

I noticed Rex watching silently, his expression curious and somewhat sad. "You okay?" I asked him.

He nodded. "I'm fine." He looked up at me. "I'm not going to say that I regret who I am because, frankly, that's not me." Rex turned to watch his sister standing next to her werewolf mate several feet within the boundary. "But this boundary? This is the second time I've felt cut off from my sister because of a witch ward. I don't like it. If she needed me…"

I nodded, not knowing what else to say.

"Okay, it's time," Althea announced, and we moved to different vantage points around the fire, not speaking. "If everyone could keep their trap shut, please, that would help. I need to concentrate."

Damien sat up. "What if I have a—"

"Dude, if you don't think I have a potion that will shut you up whether you want to or not, you are sorely underestimating the things I brought in my little black bag," Althea told him coldly. "Lay down, and keep quiet."

Damien paused and then resumed his position on the ground.

Ayla walked over to the table and sorted through the bottles, choosing some and tossing others aside. Eddie approached her, looking over her shoulder. Emma hovered near the clearing's edge as if she was afraid to get any closer.

Althea knelt down next to Damien and Ivy, who were looking at each other with a mix of apprehension and fear in their eyes. "This is going to hurt," she warned Ivy, "but it will only last for a few minutes. I promise."

Althea then took Damien's hand in hers and sliced open his wrist with a knife. Ayla stepped forward and poured various colors of potions around them both as his blood began to flow. Althea did the same to Ivy's wrist, slightly wincing as the young woman's blood mixed with Damien's on the ground.

We all stood there silently watching as the two bled out, the colors of the potions swirling around them and mixing like a kaleidoscope. Ivy's body began to jerk and convulse after a few seconds, and she cried out in pain. Ayla reacted quickly, splattering multicolored liquid from glowing bottles directly on Ivy to calm her transition.

Farah instinctively reached for the girl, but Althea grabbed her arm, holding her back. "You can't help her," she said sharply. "This is something she has to do on her own. Don't break the circle!"

It was hard to watch.

Damien looked frightened, but Ivy looked petrified. Her bleeding arm was swollen and pink as the vampire infection raced through her body toward the opening Althea had created for it to escape. My sister stared intently at that arm, her eyes weighing the progress of her ritual.

"We're almost there," she whispered. "Just a little further."

My phone buzzed in my pocket. I pulled it out and saw a text from Jason.

Is everything okay?

I put it back in my pocket without answering.

"Now, Ayla!" Althea and Ayla dumped goopy, neon-colored liquid from bottles on the blood that had pooled between Ivy and Damien. It immediately smoked and boiled.

"What the—" Damien yelped and tried to get up, but Althea pushed him back down.

"No, you idiot! You'll ruin everything! Just stay still!" she yelled at him.

The air around them shimmered and distorted. Ayla stepped back, her face a mask of concentration. Emma edged closer, her eyes wide with wonder.

Ivy was shaking uncontrollably now, her body arching off the ground as if in extreme pain. Her mouth was open in a silent scream, and her eyes were rolled back in her head so that only the whites were visible.

And then, suddenly, it was over.

Just like that.

The vampire blood receded back into Damien's veins, and Ivy's skin turned from pale white to a very healthy human-looking pink. She collapsed back onto the ground, gasping for breath as Damien sat up slowly, looking dazed but otherwise unharmed.

He looked down at his suddenly healed arm and then around the clearing. "What...what happened?"

Ivy was still lying on the ground, but she was no longer convulsing. Her arm looked normal again, albeit a little reddish. Ayla helped her sit up.

"You did it!" Ayla told her, hugging her tightly. "You're human again!"

As she looked down at herself, Ivy's eyes widened in disbelief. She ran her hand over her arm as if she half expected to feel vampire blood coursing through her veins. She looked up at Althea with tears in her eyes when she didn't.

"Thank you," she whispered.

Althea nodded and stood up. She looked around at all of us. "And that's how you reverse a half-vampire," Althea said with a smirk, dusting off her hands. "Who's the super witch now, huh?"

CHAPTER NINETEEN

*A*lthea's long locks cascaded behind her slender form like a horse's mane in the wind. She moved with an air of self-assurance toward the car, striding boldly with a defiant fierceness that seemed to replace her customary teen arrogance.

To be honest, she had every right to it. Althea, with help, had done it. She had actually reversed the half-vampire transformation. Ivy was human again.

It had been a bizarre night. As I went over the peculiar events, one thing above all others stuck out. Something surprising. The strangest thing happened as we prepared to go.

I mean the *strangest* thing.

Really out there.

Damien kept looking down at his hands as if he half expected them to grow claws or fangs or flowers or something. However, nothing happened. His arm had healed, and he was back to his normal bitter self.

Only he didn't look bitter.

As he looked up at Althea packing away her potion bottles, his eyes were filled with mournful hope. "Is there any way to reverse it for me too?" he asked pleadingly.

You could have knocked me over with an owl feather.

My sister looked surprised, and to her credit, she didn't laugh at him. But she shook her head. "I'm sorry, Damien, but once you're turned, and you've completed that transition, there's no going back. You're a vampire now, and you will be for the rest of your...um, life."

Damien hung his head in defeat as Rex watched him.

No one said anything more.

"That was weird, right?" Ayla said later from the passenger seat. "Damien's desire to be turned human again. Like, normally, I see things coming, right? But I didn't see that one coming at all. I never would have guessed."

"Super weird," Althea said from the back seat. She twisted to look back at Damien and Farah through the window. "It was like he had a sudden change of heart or something. He went from being this evil vampire to wanting to be human again all because of the magic of my ritual."

Well, no lack of confidence there.

"Maybe all that bluff and bluster and cruelty was a cover. Maybe he was searching for something more, even if he didn't know what it was," I mused, turning onto Main Street. "Maybe seeing what we all did for Ivy—and what she did for herself—gave him another perspective, made him realize what he really needed to find peace." I frowned. "Which is unfortunate since he can't have it."

As we considered that possibility, we all fell silent. It was a sad thought, but not entirely unthinkable—and, honestly, I couldn't be depressed. It was a good night, despite Damien's disappointing realization at the end.

Ivy returned home immediately after the ritual, eager to show her mother she was once again the human daughter she remembered. Ayla reported that Killian/Kevin followed her home, and I hoped the family—living and dead—could work through what had taken place so they all could heal.

Eddie and Emma decided to walk home so they could discuss the upcoming change in their family status. "We'll meet you back at Arden House," Emma promised me. "It won't take too long."

Farah had watched Damien with fascinated curiosity as the vampire seemed to plunge into a regretful depression right there in the clearing. Much to my surprise, the vampire retributionist did not immediately decapitate him when I reported Ami texted me that the star card was no longer glowing and Farah could, at any time, do her will without interference from me.

After a few minutes, Ayla spoke up again.

"It makes you wonder what other regrets people are hiding deep down, doesn't it? And if they'll ever get the chance to correct them before it's too late."

"I don't know," I said slowly. "It seems to me that sometimes people are meant to live with their regrets. Maybe it's not such a bad thing. It makes them who they are, after all." Regrets lived within me, and yes, sometimes, they were painful. (And sometimes they walked up to you as a vampire.) But they also lit the pathways that my life took, one thing leading to another.

Even if I regretted many things, I couldn't regret where I'd wound up.

Ayla was silent for a moment, contemplating my words. "Maybe you're right," she said finally. "But I still can't help but feel sorry for Damien. I get the feeling he's going to be stuck with his regret for a very long time."

"Not long at all if Farah does the deed," Althea countered from the back seat.

"Will she, though?" Ayla asked no one in particular. "Aunt Gertie says that she and Damien are going back to Ivy's house to apologize. Maybe Farah's retribution is going in a different direction this time. It doesn't have to be death. Retribution is just punishment inflicted on someone as vengeance. Maybe she has another plan."

She did indeed—and none of us would have ever guessed it, psychic though we all were.

But that's a story for another time.

* * *

"Can I talk to you?" Jason asked a few minutes after we finished filling everyone in. Mom, Ami, and Aunt Gwennie had beamed with so much pride they could have supernova-ed a star into existence. Um…out of existence?

Anyway, they were very proud of Althea.

"Sure. Porch talk?" I offered.

"Okay," he said, heading for the back of the house.

"So, I was sort of wondering," he began when we were seated on the porch swing, "why you didn't come to get me before going out to Cassandra?"

Why didn't I come to get him? "I don't know. You didn't really have a role to play in the ritual, and we only had my Jeep." I shrugged. "I just didn't think to do it."

I didn't know how to answer because I wasn't sure where this question was coming from. I waited for the next question because the look on his face told me another one was coming.

"And my text. You never answered my text."

Oh, crap.

I had forgotten about his text.

"I didn't…um, look at it." It was the first thing I could think of to say, and I felt instantly guilty because it was a total lie. I did remember seeing his text in the middle of the ritual, and I could have answered it, but I didn't have time to deal with it.

Because you were standing there doing nothing? Archie's voice faintly echoed in my mind. I didn't know if it was real or my guilty conscience conjuring the bird's sarcastic judgment, but either way, it was spot on.

"Was there a reason you didn't look at my text?" he asked, staring hard at me.

"Well, you know," I said, trying to think up a good excuse as I dug myself in deeper and deeper. "Things were kind of hectic."

"Hectic," he repeated. "Too hectic to type a couple of words out to let me know that you were okay." The tension, subtle though it was, rolled off my boyfriend in waves. "I was worried. I was completely dependent on your mother, aunts, and sister to let me know what was going on." He tilted his head. "That didn't feel good."

I should have known better. "Look, I'm sorry." We shared a look, and I saw that he wasn't mad or anything. Just disappointed. "It's just a habit from my time in the military, I guess. We stay focused on the mission until the mission is done. I was so focused on doing what I needed to do for the good of everyone involved that I didn't even consider anyone else's feelings—your feelings. I'm sorry, Jason."

"I guess," he said finally, still looking at me, but the disappointment seemed to fade. "It's not that big of a deal, I know. I mean, once I knew you were okay, I wasn't that worried anymore."

I let out a breath of relief, relieved that he wasn't mad, relieved that he understood, relieved that he would not hold a grudge or anything. "Really?"

"Well, yeah. I mean, I trust you." Jason smiled at me. "I shouldn't have said anything, and I'm sorry I did."

"No, it's okay," I interrupted, my guilt causing a cascade of corrective words. I just lied to the guy, I left him out, I ignored him, and he was apologizing. It made me feel even worse. "I was an ass. I should have picked up the phone and texted back. It would have taken, like, two seconds. I mean, if I can organize the reversal of a half-vampire back to human and stop a vampire apocalypse, I should be able to return a damn text."

"True." Jason laughed softly, and the tension that had sat between us just a moment ago dissolved. "I've been feeling really distant from you lately. Look, Astra," he said, turning. "I know you're a goddess-chosen witch with a past history I probably won't ever understand, and I'm just a middle school teacher from a small Florida town—"

"Jason," I broke in. "You're kind, funny, handsome, and sweet. You're also compassionate, and you have a heart of gold. You're smart, talented, and good at what you do. You have a really big heart, and you're hard-working and responsible. You're the whole package. You're not just a middle school teacher."

He smiled wryly. "See? You get me."

I rolled my eyes. "And I'm not just saying that because you're my boyfriend, either. It's the truth."

"That's just it. I don't feel like your boyfriend sometimes," Jason admitted. He shifted on the swing and looked into my eyes, his face serene but serious. "You've been chosen and have a job that's important on top of that, and I get that. And I get balancing relationships and work, and commitments like these can be hard—"

"But?" I asked, not liking the way this conversation was going.

"But I feel like...I feel like you, and I are always an afterthought," he replied seriously. "I'm not just hanging around because I have nothing better to do with my time and no one better to spend it with for the moment. I want to be here because you want me to be here. At least, I think you do. Because you care about me. Because I'm important to you."

"I do want you here, Jason," I said as sincerely as I could. "I do care about you."

"But?" he asked, a half-grin on his face.

"I want to be with you," I replied slowly. "But I also want to do what I was born to do. I'm not saying I don't enjoy our time together, but there's a lot of responsibility that comes with being what I am, and it comes first."

"And I understand that," he assured quickly. "I do, and I wouldn't try to change you. I'm actually really proud of you and the way you're dealing with all of it. You're doing really, really well."

"Thanks," I said, smiling.

"But...I guess what I'm saying is that I love you," he said, taking my hand.

I froze.

Bomb dropped.

Shots fired.

Danger, Will Robinson, Danger.

He said it.

Jason was—unintentionally—making me feel really guilty, which technically wasn't entirely necessary. If I stopped to think about it, I already realized I was doing a pretty bad job of balancing my own life, my commitments, and my relationship with him. He always came last. I didn't mean to do it; it just kind of…happened.

Now that he threw the L-word into this?

I felt about a thousand times worse for it.

"I don't know if I'm ready to say that back yet."

"I know," Jason said, his voice soft. He didn't sound sad, though.

"I'm not saying I don't *feel* that way, Jason," I said as sincerely as I could without actually using that four-letter word. "I do care about you. You're everything I said. You're so much more, too. But I'm a witch and a goddess-chosen whatever the heck, and that's really all I can be sometimes. It's who I am. Sometimes I wish I didn't have to be that way. Sometimes I wish I could just be Astra, the woman you're dating, the almost middle-aged woman who l—cares about you who's just looking to land a man and settle down."

"But?" he asked.

There were an awful lot of buts in this conversation.

"But I'm not meant to be that woman," I explained. "I'm meant to be the woman who stops vampires from ruling the world. I'm meant to be the woman who's sometimes in danger, sometimes in a rush, sometimes in a hurry. I'm meant to be the woman who does what she has to do to make sure things are taken care of."

"But you're also Astra," he said softly. "You're not just a witch or a goddess-chosen whatever. You're the woman who's sitting here on this swing with me. You're also the woman who helped bring an innocent back from the brink of darkness. Most of all, to me, you're the woman who's made me feel better than I have felt in a really long time."

I stared at him silently, unsure of what to say.

"I'm not asking you to give up anything, Astra," he said, his eyes never leaving mine. "I'm just asking you to make room for me. No rush."

"Okay," I replied quietly.

"And it's okay if you say you're not ready to say *it* back," he said, that half-smile on his face again as he avoided saying the L-word. "You can say it back when you're ready. No rush, and no pressure."

"Okay," I repeated, smiling at him.

"But I hope you will," he added, winking at me.

"Yeah. Me, too," I agreed.

And I think I meant it.

"Now," Jason said, standing. "I'm starving. How about I go make us something to eat."

"Okay," I agreed, still not moving from my swing.

"You want to stay here?" he asked.

"Yeah," I said. "I'll be right in."

* * *

I HAD a feeling Archie was nearby, watching the exchange, and sure enough, as soon as the back door closed, the owl swooped down onto the porch and looked up at me with his dark eyes. "So, you want me to distract you with news, or do you want to talk about it?"

"I don't know," I admitted. "I don't know what I want."

"Not for nothing, but that was obvious. You could go inside and make out with him," he suggested. "Maybe that will help shake loose whatever crazy blockage is in your brain."

"Archie!"

Archie cocked his head to the side. "Astra!"

. . .

I WASN'T sure I wanted to talk about it, but I also felt I had to. "He says he loves me," I said, swinging gently. "And that he doesn't want me to give up anything—he just wants me to make room for him. Which is reasonable." I paused. "And it's a reasonable request." I paused again.

Archie stood on the porch a moment, looking at me, and suddenly, I felt very much like I was the one under his scrutiny. "Uh-huh."

"What? What is that very judgmental expression?" I asked.

"My face." Archie tilted his head to the side. "You lied to him. You saw that text. You slipped your phone back in your pocket so fast—"

"I know I did! I know. Yes. I did." I said defensively. "And I had a good reason, I thought. I didn't want to hurt his feelings. I didn't want to tell him I didn't really care at that moment if he was worried. I mean, how do you admit something like that? It's wrong. I know it's wrong. I was wrong." I looked out at the stars twinkling in the sky and the moon overhead. "I swear, the military was easy. Clear objectives. Clear understandings. Everyone was in the same boat, everyone knowing what was what. Tunnel vision was a good thing."

"You're not an uncaring jerk, Astra. You

made a mistake." Archie sat down on the porch beside me and took a moment to groom his feathers.

"That wasn't a mistake. A mistake is tripping over a curb. Not caring that he was worried? That's old tapes playing. I focused on the objective for my entire adult life. I didn't care about feelings. Mine or anyone else's." I wasn't supposed to. I sighed again. "This? This is just… really hard. Harder than I thought it would be.

"Which part?"

"All of it," I replied. Then I considered further and said, "Well, most of it. And I swear, Jason's too understanding. If I'm not careful, I'm going to walk all over him."

"There's a complaint you don't hear every day."

I sighed again. "I'm not good at this relationship stuff. I've never done it before. Not out here in a semi-normal world. I don't know how to prioritize this."

"So, work at it. I'm all ears. Well, I'm more eyes than ears if we want to get technical. But I have ears. I can listen," Archie said. "Let's talk this through. WE can figure it out."

"Not tonight. I'm too tired." I sighed. "Distract me."

Archie hopped onto the swing. "Emma and Eddie worked things out."

"That's great."

"He's moving here."

I smiled. "I think that'll be good for her. It'll be better for them if they try and work stuff out. And I hope they do. I think they'd make a good couple. She just needs to get over her paranormal reactionary thing."

Archie coughed. "With his pack."

I sat up and blinked. "What? What with his pack?"

"He's moving to town *with his pack*. It's a dozen or so wolves, I think."

"Huh," I said, trying to process through the shock. "That's...unexpected."

"Yeah," Archie admitted, bobbing his head a little. "I think it's a good thing, though. I think it'll give him a place to belong. Eddie's been trying to belong his whole life. Emma, too. They're good for one another."

"But a whole werewolf pack?" I asked. "Here in Forkbridge?"

"Maybe it'll turn out to be the best thing ever," Archie suggested. "We should welcome them. It would certainly be better than the reaction you gave me when I got here."

"I didn't give you a reaction," I objected.

"Two lies in one night!" Archie exclaimed and flapped his wings. "You most certainly did. I was told to leave. In between insults."

"Well," I said, "I didn't kick you or anything." Archie's expression told me that wasn't much of a comfort.

"It's fine. I forgive you. You were upset."

I sighed. "I was."

Archie and I sat in silence for a while, contemplating the news of the werewolf pack moving in. It was a lot to take in, and I wasn't sure how to feel about it.

I was…torn.

On the one hand, I was happy for Emma. She deserved to be happy and to find someone who loved her as much as Eddie did.

But on the other hand, a werewolf pack? In Forkbridge? Where were they going to stay, in the vampire B&B? I rubbed my eyes and sighed again.

It seemed like a recipe for disaster.

"It's not like they all run around in wolf form all the time," Archie said. "They're mostly normal, if very furry, looking people. And they're all richer than King Midas, so maybe it will be good for the town. Well, not Eddie. Eddie's not rich."

The owl tilted his head. "But kind of Eddie, because he's the pack leader."

"Do you think they'll fit in?" I asked finally.

"I don't know," Archie replied. "But do any of us really?"

I nodded and stood up. "Okay," I said. "Let's go welcome the new pack to town."

"Awesome. We can talk about your boyfriend problems after." Archie flapped his wings once more, bobbing up and down a little. "I'm glad I was assigned to you. Things just keep getting more interesting around here."

That they do.

* * *

THANK YOU FOR READING!

I hope you enjoyed Against Owl Odds. Please think about leaving a review! Astra, Archie and the whole Arden family continue their adventures in Book 9, Owl Spell Broke Loose.

KEEP UP WITH LEANNE LEEDS

Thanks so much for reading! I hope you liked it! Want to keep up with me?

Visit leanneleeds.com to:

Find all my books...

Sign up for my newsletter...

Like me on Facebook...

Follow me on Twitter...

Follow me on Instagram...

Thanks again for reading!

Leanne Leeds

FIND A TYPO? LET US KNOW!

Typos happen. It's sad, but true.

Though we go over the manuscript multiple times, have editors, have beta readers, and advance readers it's inevitable that determined typos and mistakes sometimes find their way into a published book.

Did you find one? If you did, think about reporting it on leanneleeds.com so we can get it corrected.

Printed in Great Britain
by Amazon

17916785R00194